Their gazes met and locked.

Sexual awareness flared in all its heat and glory, stirring up something more powerful than words. Seeing that was making Matt forget the shackles of guilt he hadn't been able to shake.

For a moment, he almost felt whole again—as if that accident had never happened.

He knew he ought to say something, but he didn't want her to get the wrong idea and think that they were actually creating some kind of friendship or bond.

Tori was too attractive.

Too appealing.

And pretending otherwise was only going to mess with his mind.

Dear Reader,

June is one of my favorite months of the year. The school year is winding down, and the days are growing warmer and longer. It's time for sunny afternoons at the shore and family barbecues in the backyard.

It's also time for vacations. The Duarte family will be going to Colorado Springs again this month. And at the end of July, I'll be heading for San Francisco. How about you? Do you have plans to travel? Or will you just kick back and spend a few lazy summer days at home?

Either way, I'm glad you decided to read Matt and Tori's story, *In Love with the Bronc Rider,* which is the second book in THE TEXAS HOMECOMING series. As some of you may have guessed, I believe in second chances and new beginnings. So you'll see both in this story.

Happy reading!

Judy

IN LOVE WITH
THE BRONC RIDER

JUDY DUARTE

SPECIAL EDITION®

Published by Silhouette Books

America's Publisher of Contemporary Romance

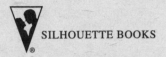

SILHOUETTE BOOKS

ISBN-13: 978-0-373-24907-7
ISBN-10:   0-373-24907-1

IN LOVE WITH THE BRONC RIDER

This edition published by arrangement with Harlequin Books S.A.

® and TM are trademarks of Harlequin Books S.A., used under license.
Trademarks indicated with ® are registered in the United States Patent
and Trademark Office, the Canadian Trade Marks Office and in other
countries.

Visit Silhouette Books at www.eHarlequin.com

Printed in U.S.A.

JUDY DUARTE

always knew there was a book inside her, but since English was her least favorite subject in school, she never considered herself a writer. An avid reader who enjoys a happy ending, Judy couldn't shake the dream of creating a book of her own.

Her dream became a reality in March of 2002, when Silhouette Special Edition released her first book, *Cowboy Courage*. Since then, she has sold nineteen more novels. And in July of 2005, Judy won a prestigious Readers' Choice Award for *The Rich Man's Son*.

Judy makes her home near the beach in Southern California. When she's not cooped up in her writing cave, she's spending time with her somewhat enormous, but delightfully close family.

You can write to Judy c/o Silhouette Books, 233 Broadway, Suite 1001, New York, NY 10237. You can also contact her at JudyDuarte@sbcglobal.net or through her Web site, www.judyduarte.com.

IN MEMORY OF:

Mahnita Boyden-Wofford, who went above and beyond the call of duty by taking such good care of her boss, his wife and a slew of kids and grandkids.

"I'm not family," you used to say, "I just work here." But that couldn't have been any further from the truth.

May God bless and keep you until we meet again.

Chapter One

Tori McKenzie slapped her hands on her denim-clad hips and studied the twenty-six-year-old man sitting before her, defiance etched in bold strokes across his handsome face.

She'd taken all she could stand from Matthew Clayton, and even a softie like her was bound to explode sometime. "Are you immune to the feelings of others? You've made the poor cook cry three times this week. And she doesn't deserve it."

The afternoon sun slanting through the window highlighted strands of gold in Matt's uncombed, chestnut-colored hair. If he'd been going for the rugged, sexy look, his tousled locks and unshaven appearance would be enough to cause a flock of buckle bunnies to swoon.

But Tori knew better than that. Matt didn't seem to care about anything these days. Not even his appearance.

If she hadn't been a registered nurse once upon a time and sworn to promote healing, she would have ditched this thankless assignment the moment Granny—Tori's employer and Matt's sweet, elderly mother—had suggested it.

As it was, now she was stuck trying to get through to the stubborn man who refused to let anyone break down the walls he'd put up.

"I just want to be left alone," he said. "Can't you and the cook get that through your pretty little heads?"

Tori wasn't prone to violence, particularly when the target was a man who'd been confined to a wheelchair following a tragic car accident, but she had a growing compulsion to grab him by the scruff of his shirt and shake some sense into him.

Instead she muttered, "A lot you know."

Matt relaxed his rebellious pose, allowing himself to sit easier in that chair than a former rodeo cowboy ought to. "Now, listen here, Red—"

"Don't call me Red." He couldn't know that the childhood taunt still rubbed her the wrong way, and telling him might actually make his mood worse, but her patience had run thin today. "You have no idea how old that nickname has gotten or what negative connotations it holds for me. Call me Tori. Or Ms. McKenzie, if you prefer."

"All right." He crossed his arms over his chest. "Then Miz McKenzie it is. But either way, I'm still not interested in your help or your sympathy. And you can pass that info on to Connie, too. She was hired to cook, and you signed on to clean the house and do laundry—not babysit me. So go peddle your damn TLC elsewhere."

"I have nowhere else to peddle it." And that was the truth. Tori had left her job at the hospital and had no intention of applying for another position elsewhere—at least, not in the near future.

Nor was she ready to provide references and offer any explanations.

She wasn't sure what had gone down in her personnel file after her brother's foolish crime, but she'd been officially reprimanded about it.

And the entire situation had been embarrassing—painfully so.

Someday she'd go back to nursing, she supposed. But right now, she was still licking her wounds.

"Well, I don't need your golly-gee, everything's-turning-up-roses attitude," Matt said. "So why don't you find something else to do and leave me alone?"

"Because I need your help."

His brow furrowed and his right eye twitched. "What do you want *me* to do? Reach something for you? Maybe run out to the barn and saddle a horse so you can go out riding?"

"Actually," she said, "your mother's birthday is coming up in a few weeks. And I need help planning a party."

He blew out a snortlike breath. "I don't *do* parties."

"She's going to be eighty." Tori made her way toward his wheelchair, as though they'd broached some kind of friendship when that couldn't be any further from the truth. "And you and I are going to figure out a way to surprise her."

"Good luck with that. People in town have been trying to plan celebrations behind her back for as long as I can remember, and she always catches wind of it. No one surprises Granny."

"You and I will."

He reached over to the lamp table and took a glass of amber-colored liquid, which could be either melted-down iced tea or whiskey.

She suspected it was the latter, although she couldn't be sure unless she got close enough to catch a whiff of his breath.

"I told you before," he said. "I don't *do* parties."

"And I told *you,* Granny is going to be eighty in a few weeks. That's a very big deal. Do you realize this could be the last birthday party she ever has?"

"Don't say that!" His words came out sharp, abrupt. And his response was the first sign of any tender feelings he might have bottled up with all that grief he'd undoubtedly suppressed.

Good. That meant she was making progress. So she was glad she'd thrown out her ace in the hole—his deep love for and devotion to the woman who'd raised him.

Granny had been a childless widow who was pushing sixty when she adopted Jared, her oldest son. Matt, the youngest, had come next, followed a year later by Greg, whom Tori had never met.

The homeless boys hadn't had any kind of future to look forward to when Granny had opened her heart and her home to them. And as a result, they each loved her unconditionally.

Tori got behind Matt and began to push his wheelchair, just as she'd been pushing him emotionally for the past few minutes, pressing him to do what was best for him.

"What in the hell do you think you're doing?" he asked.

"Taking you outside."

"And *then* what are you planning to do? Push me down the steps?"

"Would you blame me if I did?"

He grunted as though he knew how difficult he could be, how miserable he'd become to anyone who got within five feet of him.

"The foreman had a couple of the ranch hands build a ramp from the mudroom into the yard so that you can get in and out easier." She didn't dare admit that the men had done so at her request.

"What if I don't want to get in and out?" He turned his neck, glancing over his shoulder at her. His gaze locked on hers as she continued taking him where he didn't want to go. "Did you hear what I said? I don't *want* to go outside."

"You don't seem to give a darn about anyone else's feelings around here," she said, catching a whiff of alcohol on his breath. "Why should I care about yours?"

"Because you're a pushy little thing. Did anyone ever tell you that you remind them of a bantam rooster when you get your feathers ruffled?"

"No. But thank you. I do believe that's more accurate than what you called me yesterday."

"You mean carrot top?"

"Carrot tops are green."

"So they are."

She'd been warned that he could be especially surly and ornery when he drank, so she'd have to keep that in mind as she chipped away at his barriers. She might have pushed him too hard today already, but she couldn't very well backpedal now.

In the kitchen she stopped long enough to open the plastic

container in which Connie, the new cook, kept the leftover goodies and sweets she'd made, and Tori grabbed two chocolate chip cookies, handing one to Matt. Then she continued to take him through the mudroom to the back door.

As she began to steer him down the wooden planks the ranch hands had built, the slope and his weight caused the chair to pick up momentum. "Uh-oh."

He grabbed for the top of the wheels with hands that still bore the calluses of a man who'd worked with cattle and horses all his life. His efforts crushed the cookie she'd given him a moment ago. "Dammit, Tori. Are you trying to kill me?"

"Actually, the thought crossed my mind earlier, but I suspect Granny would like to have you around, at least until her birthday." Tori continued along the dirt pathway to the barn.

"Where do you think you're taking me?"

"I have an idea for the party, and I want to get your thoughts on it."

"I don't see why. You seem hell-bent on having your own way no matter what I say."

Actually, she was hoping that the fresh air and sunshine would brighten his mood. That maybe, if he were able to inhale the familiar smells of the ranch, the animals, the alfalfa and oats, he'd remember what he'd liked about life—before the accident had taken all he loved away from him.

Jared had said that Matt had been a rodeo cowboy, that he'd always enjoyed life and had lived it to the fullest. But after the accident that had crushed his legs and killed his fiancée and her young son, Matt no longer cared whether he lived or died. And apparently, that meant he didn't care if he walked again, either.

According to Jared, Matt's doctor had wanted him to start physical therapy, but for some reason he'd chosen not to.

So the nurse in Tori was determined to pull him out of the blue funk he'd slipped into, even if it was the last thing she did.

Sometimes life dealt a sucky blow to people—or sometimes more than that, as it had to her. And a person just had to make the best of it.

She pushed Matt through the open doorway into the barn, where the scent of oats and horse and leather was especially strong. A couple of broodmares and their colts were stabled along the side walls.

"What are we doing in here?" Matt asked.

"Checking out the setting of the party."

"You can't be serious. You want to have a party in the barn?"

"Well, we could at least hide the people in here." She studied the interior. "You have to admit, it limits the amount of decorating we'd need to do if we chose a cowboy theme. Hey, what do you think about hiring a country-western band?"

He scoffed. "And how about pony rides for all the guests? And maybe a piñata filled with candy under the tree in the front yard."

She wondered what his voice actually sounded like without the ever-present surly tone. She really didn't know the real Matt. Only that he'd been a rising star on the rodeo circuit and could no longer compete because of his injuries.

"I'd like to surprise Granny," she said. "And where better than right under her nose? She goes to church each Sunday. We could have everyone arrive after she leaves. We can hide the vehicles, then set up all the food in here. I think we can pull it off."

"If you're dead set on having it at the ranch, why not have it out near the lake?"

"Ooh. That's an even better idea. I'm glad you thought of it." She scanned the barn again. "We can give people a ride on a buckboard to the lake."

"A buckboard? What the hell are you talking about? We don't have a buckboard."

"Maybe we can rent one."

"From where?"

"Hmmm." She put the tip of her index finger into her mouth and lightly bit down on it. Then she cocked her head to the side. "I don't know. But I'm sure you'll think of something. Put that on your list of things to do."

He grimaced, but didn't say no.

"And if we have it by the lake, we'll also need to rent portable potties. You can be in charge of getting those, too."

"Okay, now you're *really* getting out of hand."

A horse whinnied, and Tori turned toward it. "Oh, look. How sweet is that? A mom and its baby."

She made her way to the stall and stroked the mother's velvety nose. She'd always been a city girl, and all of this was new to her. But if she had to give up her old life, at least the new one wasn't completely intolerable.

"Her name is Willow," Matt said. "And she's one of the best cutting horses Granny has."

"She's cute."

"Horses aren't cute."

"I think they are." She turned, leaning her hip against the stall. "Or were you referring to the jackass on the premises? You know, the one who snaps at anyone trying to reach out to him?"

Touché. So she thought he was an ass. That served his purpose.

Instead of conjuring a snappy retort, Matt studied the pesky redhead, with her wild curly hair and eyes that were as green as anything the Emerald Isle had to offer. He could almost imagine her speaking with a bit of the brogue, although there was an intriguing lilt in her voice as it was.

Either way, she promised to be the death of him, but only because he hadn't been able to run her off, like he had Connie, the cook. A part of him felt a bit of remorse at having made Connie cry, but not enough to change his tune.

He wasn't in the mood to socialize and hadn't been since the accident. Why couldn't people just leave him alone?

For that reason he made one last attempt to get Tori off his back. "I heard a rumor about you and want to know if it's true."

She tucked a loose strand of hair behind her ear. "What did you hear?"

He hadn't believed what Jared had said about her background. After all, why would she be stuck out on this ranch, getting a small wage plus room and board, if she had other options?

But his older brother didn't spread tales.

For one guilty moment Matt considered changing course by making up something that would provide some comic relief. But he reminded himself that even though he'd told her to leave him alone, she hadn't been sensitive to his need for privacy. So why should he care about hers?

"I heard that you used to be a nurse," he said. "Before you became a maid."

She stilled to the point that a light breeze might blow her off balance, a reaction that told him what he'd heard was true. And he figured a career change like that hadn't been made on a whim.

Not that there was anything wrong with being a maid. But people didn't usually put aside years of training and education without having a good reason to do so, and it made him wonder just what hers was.

"Why'd you give it up?" he asked. "I would imagine there's always a need for nurses."

She seemed to stew on her answer.

Or maybe she was suffering over it. It was hard to say.

Her stance softened. "Let's just say that there have been a lot of changes in my life."

Apparently so, but it only made Matt all the more curious about her.

"Have you seen the kittens?" she asked, changing the subject.

"No, I haven't." He ought to keep chipping away at her, but then again, he had his own demons and secrets, so maybe he should respect hers.

She turned her back to him, and in spite of his efforts to shun both her and her feminine attributes, he couldn't help watching the sway of her hips as she walked toward an empty stall.

Tori McKenzie was a pretty woman. And even though

Matt had teased her about the color of her hair, it wasn't because he didn't find it attractive.

Cindy Wilson, his fiancée, had paid to have hers dyed that same color, which he suspected was natural in Tori's case.

In fact, Tori reminded him a lot of Cindy, at least in looks. She wasn't nearly as tall, but she was just as pretty. Maybe even more so.

And that was another reason to keep his distance. He didn't need the constant reminder of the woman who'd died. A woman who would still be alive today if it hadn't been for Matt's stubborn streak and competitive spirit.

Not a day went by that Matt didn't blame himself for his fiancée's death—her son's, too. And he'd never be the same man again.

In more ways than one.

Damn, he missed the rodeo.

"The kitties are right over here," Tori said. "Joey told me where to find them. And I've been checking on them each day for him."

Joey was the bookkeeper's nephew, a six-year-old kid who'd had heart surgery a week ago and was now recovering at Jared's ranch.

Matt could hear the sound of friction and shuffling, as Tori moved something away. A box, maybe. Then she stepped out of the shadows and back into plain sight, where she stooped, providing him with a vision of her perfectly rounded backside.

His hormones stirred, letting him know that there was still a healthy young man lurking inside of him. A man capable of feeling again—if he would only allow himself to.

But to be honest? Matt wasn't sure if that was a good thing or not.

Part of him wanted to waste away in an effort to find peace and resolution. Yet he knew that really wasn't going to help. He feared he was stuck with the remorse and grief forever.

A flurry of mews and meows sounded from where Tori was bent, and when she returned, she carried a tiny gray tabby with white markings. Its eyes hadn't been open long.

"This is Boswell," she said.

"You named it?"

"Of course." She placed the kitten against her cheek, allowing the fur to caress her skin. "Why wouldn't I?"

"It's just a barn cat."

She turned the kitten's face to hers and whispered, "Matt makes being a barn kitty sound like a bad thing, Boswell. But you're precious, aren't you?"

Crazy woman. Cindy had been like that, too—a real animal lover.

Tori handed the kitten to Matt, and even though he didn't want to take it from her, he accepted the small ball of fur. It wasn't cute, of course, as she'd claimed. Instead he thought it resembled a baby rat.

He supposed he could understand why she thought differently, though. She was like his mother—at least, in that one respect.

Granny had instantly zeroed in on the potential she'd seen in Matt and his brothers, the possibilities that could take place if they were given some time to grow and a whole lot of nurturing.

Of course, homeless adolescents with big chips on their shoulders weren't at all what most women would call "cute." And they weren't as easy to raise as a kitten was. So Matt knew better than to think Tori was anywhere near as admirable as the woman who'd taken him into her heart and home.

Boswell mewed, although it was actually more like a cry of distress.

"Here." Matt handed the kitten back to Tori. "He wants to be with his mother and his brothers and sisters."

In fact, Matt realized, the mama cat must've been out scrounging for a meal, because it struck him odd that she wasn't whining and carrying on about the loss of one of her babies.

"There are six of these little guys in the litter," Tori said. "Joey is going to take the orange tabby, as well as the gray-and-white one."

"Has anyone considered whether they're males or females? We'll need to know if we place an ad in the paper to give them away."

Tori paused, then turned it over and looked at its belly. "This one's a girl, I guess. So maybe I'd better think of a different name. Boswell isn't very feminine."

Obviously, she figured it was as easy to determine the sex of cats as it was dogs. And Matt knew better.

"Let me take a look at it."

She handed it back, and Matt looked under the tail. "This one's a boy. So the name Boswell shouldn't cause him any trouble with his feline peers."

"It can't be a boy. He doesn't have a…" She paused and their gazes locked.

A smile tugged at Matt's lips. "Oh, yes he does. It's just not as evident as it is on dogs or horses or cattle."

Or on humans.

His grin widened. Damn. When was the last time he'd smiled?

It felt like forever, but he hadn't found anything even remotely entertaining since the hours prior to the accident. And actually, considering the way events had unfolded that day, it had been longer than that.

Either way, a slight frown slid back into place, eliminating any sign of a smile.

Footsteps sounded, and Matt turned to see Lester, the foreman, enter the barn.

"What you got there?" Lester asked, as if he didn't have eyes and couldn't see for himself.

"Tori took a fancy to one of the kittens," Matt told him.

"Oh, yeah?" Lester lifted his hat and raked a hand through his thinning, scrub-brush hair. "How bad of a fancy?"

"What do you mean?" Tori asked.

Lester crossed his arms and shifted his weight to one booted foot. "Bad enough to bottle-feed that little critter for the next couple of weeks?"

Matt knew there wouldn't be any other reason for the foreman to ask. "What happened to the mother?"

"A coyote got a hold of her last night," Lester said. "I'm afraid she's dead."

"Those poor babies." Tori clucked her tongue. "They're too little to make it on their own, so I'll take care of them."

"That's a lot of work," Matt said.

She stiffened and stood as tall as her barely five-foot frame would allow. "Not for me."

Something told Matt that a wise man wouldn't doubt her word. And being a man who prided himself on having good sense, Matt realized he'd better brace himself for more run-ins with Tori.

Because in spite of his wishes to be elsewhere, here he sat, virtually kidnapped by an attractive redhead who didn't take no for an answer.

He watched as Tori returned the kitten to the nest it shared with its brothers and sisters. He'd lucked out when she'd determined the orphaned felines were more in need of her tender loving care than he was. After all, he was getting tired of her interference.

Yet instead of wheeling himself out of the barn and back to the house, he found himself studying her shapely backside. He couldn't help admiring the way the denim stretched across her hips.

Her blouse had pulled away from her waistband and provided a view of the fair skin of her lower back. And in spite of every lick of good sense he'd ever had, he imagined himself walking again, pain-free and without a limp. Imagined moseying closer and...

A jolt of testosterone shimmied through his veins and kicked his pulse up a notch.

Damn. Matt might be temporarily confined to a wheel-chair—and more or less resigned to limited mobility.

But there were still parts of him that were in prime working condition.

Chapter Two

Tori sat behind the wheel of the white pickup she'd borrowed from Lester and turned into the long, graveled drive of the Rocking C.

She'd driven into Brighton Valley and stopped at the feed store, where she had purchased a case of formula and two small bottles. She would do whatever it took to make sure those poor orphaned kittens survived, especially the two Joey was planning to keep.

Now she was bumping along the rutted dirt road, kicking up dust and heading toward the house.

She pulled the truck to the side of the barn, where she'd found it, parked and turned off the ignition. Then she grabbed the brown bag filled with her purchases and slid out of the driver's seat.

Eager to gather up the babies and take them inside the house, she went directly to the barn.

Just outside of the stall where the kittens were nested she found an empty box, which Lester must have put it for her to use. She appreciated his thoughtfulness and would be sure to tell him the next time she saw him.

After carrying the box to the place where the orphaned kittens lay crying and squirming, she knelt beside them. There was no way of knowing when the mama cat had fed them last, so she hoped they weren't dehydrated. She'd have to get some milk down them as soon as possible. So she put them into the box and carried them in the house.

Right now their bed was only cardboard. But as soon as she was able, she would find some soft rags to make them comfy. And later she would use a hot water bottle to keep them warm.

By the time she'd gotten into the kitchen, the babies were really rooting around and crying for food, and she had to readjust the bag she'd carried in from the truck while getting a better grip on the box to hold it steady.

She'd purchased two bottles, but could only feed one kitten at a time—unless, of course, she found someone to help.

And she had just the right someone in mind. It wouldn't hurt Matt at all to focus on something other than himself.

As she washed and prepared the bottles with the canned kitten formula, a voice from the doorway interrupted her work.

"I see you're back."

Matthew.

She turned, her gaze zeroing in on him as he sat in that

wheelchair. He was a handsome man, even unshaven and wearing a trademark scowl. And she couldn't squelch an appreciative grin.

Dang. She'd have to stay on her toes around him, so she quickly rallied. "I'm glad you're here. I need an extra pair of hands."

"You're still dead set on feeding them yourself?" he asked.

"I can't let them starve." She glanced over her shoulder at him. "And don't tell me they're just barn cats."

Matt put up his hands in mock surrender. "I wouldn't think of it."

He appeared both boyish and manly in that pose, and something in her heart stirred. Something that had very little to do with sympathy. But she tamped down every bit of sexual attraction as quickly as it rose. She'd come to Brighton Valley to get away from her problems, away from the whispers and knowing looks. So she certainly wasn't going to risk drawing attention to herself here.

She reached into the rag drawer and pulled out a couple of soft pieces for bedding. Then she took an old worn towel and tore it in two. She swaddled the orange tabby, the one Joey had been calling Pumpkin, and handed the squawking bundle, along with a bottle, to Matt.

He took it, then asked, "Why'd you wrap it up?"

"That's how we feed newborn babies. They eat better when they feel secure."

"But these are just…" He didn't finish, and she suspected he was going to say cats.

Still, it pleased her to know that he was being sensitive to her feelings about the value of these tiny creatures who hadn't been asked to be orphaned.

It didn't take long for Pumpkin to figure out what he was supposed to do with the nipple, and he soon began to chow down.

"I'll be damned," Matt said. "That nursing skill of yours seems to come in handy around here."

She stiffened, her heart thumping like dead weight against her chest wall.

Her skills had been coming in handy all right, but that didn't make her feel any better about not working in a hospital setting when she'd been trained to do so.

When Matt had asked her about being a nurse, she'd been taken aback. But not by his question or his natural curiosity about her past. It was the fact that he'd seemed to realize that she hadn't given up nursing because she'd really wanted to.

She wasn't about to confide in him, though. The memories were still too painful, too raw.

If it had been just one ugly secret, instead of two, she might have stuck it out and remained working at the hospital, hoping her brother's drug problem and theft would soon become yesterday's news. But her sister's betrayal had been a devastating blow—and completely unforgivable.

That particular incident had been the final straw, the trigger that made her turn her back on her family, as well as her career.

How could she go to work each day when everyone at the hospital, from the janitors to the chief of staff, had looked at her as though she was guilty by association.

Tori reached for the smallest kitten. It sucked a few draws from the bottle and soon lost interest.

"This one isn't eating," she said, her gaze seeking Matt's. "What do you think is wrong?"

Matt glanced up. Tori, her big green eyes laden with an overabundance of compassion, was looking at him as though he was an expert on cats, which he wasn't. But he'd lived on a working ranch long enough to learn and to accept certain laws of nature.

And, if truth be told, before he'd been lured to the rodeo circuit, he'd harbored a dream of becoming a vet. But other than an aptitude in math and science, he hadn't been that good of a student, so it had been fairly easy to decide against college.

"That's the runt," he said, knowing that the weakest one in the litter usually had an uphill battle to survive. But he knew better than to tell that to Tori. She'd probably get all weepy-eyed, and he didn't want to deal with her tears.

"He's got the cutest white markings on his feet and his nose."

Matt didn't glance her way. He was still of the mind-set that at this age, these little critters weren't much different from rats.

"Oh, and look at his tail. I'm going to call him Tippy."

Great. She'd pinned her heart on the one cat in the litter with the least chance of making it.

Damn. Matt opened his mouth to warn her, but instead of popping off with a comment she wouldn't appreciate, he held his tongue and focused on the orange tabby. He almost felt sorry for the poor thing. And not just because it had been orphaned.

To add insult to injury, Pumpkin was a lousy name for a cat. If this kitten pulled through and Matt had anything to say about it, he was going to suggest they call the little critter Rusty or Tiger or something like that.

About the time they'd fed each kitten—or at least, in the case of the runt, given it a try—Granny entered the kitchen.

"What's going on?" she asked.

Tori explained the situation. "I hope you don't mind if I try to bottle-feed these little ones until they can fend for themselves."

"Of course not," Granny said. "Joey would really be upset if anything happened to the two kittens I promised him. And I'd hate to see him brokenhearted."

So would Matt. But as his thoughts were prone to do whenever he laid eyes on Joey, they drifted to Tommy and, subsequently, to the dark, gruesome vision that would remain etched in Matt's mind for the rest of his life.

He would never forget the sight of that little boy slumped in the back seat of the dual-wheeled pickup, his body bent and twisted.

Damn. No matter how hard Matt tried, he couldn't stop the memory from marching through his brain like an enemy battalion on a mission of destruction.

"Just look at you two," Granny said, as she pulled out a chair and sat next to Tori. "You're tending those babies like doting parents, and it's just about the sweetest thing I've ever seen."

Sweet? There wasn't a damn thing sweet about any of

this. Nor was there anything wholesome about the guilt that came barreling down on Matt like two drag racers taking up both lanes of the road and leaving a man with nowhere to turn.

"You know what?" He turned to Tori. "I'm tired. And now that you've got help, I'm going to head back to my room and rest."

"Are you okay?" Tori asked.

No, he wasn't okay. And he doubted that he ever would be again.

"Yeah, I'm fine. Don't worry about me." He was trying to learn how to live with the guilt.

He just dealt with it better when no one was around.

Matt sat in his bedroom trying his damnedest to follow Captain Ahab's relentless quest for Moby Dick, and even though he was nearly three-quarters of the way through the novel and had actually found himself enjoying it, he just couldn't get back into the story.

For the past two days Tori had been drawing him out of his comfort zone, and he was beginning to feel as though she was trying to shove a tablespoon of cod liver oil down his throat.

Jared had asked Matt to stay behind at the Rocking C and keep the books for Granny while Sabrina was gone.

How could Matt say no to that?

But now he was stuck back home with Granny and the hired women who lived in the house—Connie, the cook who couldn't seem to make an edible meal if someone held a gun to her head, and Tori, a maid who looked too damn much like Cindy for comfort. And to make matters worse, neither one of the women could keep their noses out of Matt's business.

Could life be any crueler than that?

He'd managed to scare Connie off with a surly attitude, but Tori wasn't nearly as sensitive.

And if Tori didn't back off…

Well, Matt wasn't sure what he'd do. But he suspected things were going to blow sky-high.

A knock sounded on the door, interrupting his thoughts.

He wasn't up for chatter tonight—or togetherness. He just wanted some time alone.

A second rap convinced him that peace and quiet wasn't ever going to be found on the Rocking C, and he was going to have to get out of here for a while—a *long* while.

He rested the open book in his lap. "Yeah?"

"Dinner's ready," Tori said.

"Thanks," he told her through the closed door. "I'm not up for a family-style meal. I'll fix a plate and then come back in here to eat."

"Don't worry," she said. "I'll bring it to you."

That wasn't quite what he had in mind.

Moments later another knock sounded, and Tori's voice sang out. "Room service."

Matt wasn't in the mood for lighthearted banter, so he hoped she would drop off his meal without saying anything and leave him alone.

"Okay, bring it in," he told her.

As she entered the bedroom, she balanced a tray that held two plates, silverware and glasses of iced tea. "I thought I'd join you for dinner."

He ought to appreciate her presence and her attempts to take the edge off his dark thoughts, but he didn't. Sometimes it actually felt good to stew and wallow in a foul mood.

Of course, at other times, a man didn't have any choice in the matter.

Tori set the tray on the dresser, then made room on the desk for two place settings.

"What makes you think I want company?" he asked.

She turned, lips parting, cheeks flushing—and looking sweeter and prettier than he'd like her to.

"I'm sorry," she said. "It's just that you spend way too much time alone, and I thought—"

"You thought that you'd spread a little Mary Sunshine my way?"

She straightened and stared him down. The fire in those green eyes made her all the more attractive, and he struggled to right an escalating pulse rate that set his hormones on end.

"Your attitude really needs a tune-up," she said.

"Does that mean you're dead set on accepting the challenge?" He watched the billowing wind in her sails fade ever so slightly.

"You're a handsome man, Matt. That hasn't changed. And while Granny insists that all of her boys are smart as a whip, she implied you might be the brightest of all."

So what? he thought. A lot of good any of that did him now.

He'd never ride in the rodeo again; he'd never be able to bring Cindy or Tommy back.

"You have a lot to be grateful for—your life, a loving

and supportive family. Do you have any idea how many people in this world would give anything to have what you fail to see as a real blessing?"

Was she one of them? He couldn't seem to stifle the curiosity. Or the urge to turn the tables and start prying into her past for a change, poking at her pain and disappointment.

That is, if she'd ever had any.

"The life I once had is over," he said, "so you'll have to forgive me for not feeling like I ought to celebrate."

He'd expected some response—either an argument or an apology—yet she didn't offer either one.

As if he hadn't uttered a peep in retaliation, she just pointed to the book in his lap. "What are you reading?"

"Moby Dick." He glanced down at the novel he'd found in the den, a classic he suspected had once belonged to Greg or Jared. "I thought it looked…interesting."

"It is. I read it in high school. I'm not really a fan of literary fiction, but the book was assigned to the entire class, so I didn't have much choice. But it was really good. I'm sure you'll like it."

"Yeah, well, I never read any of the books I was told to read when I was in school. I'd just catch a ride with one of the ranch hands into town and pick up the Cliffs-Notes."

"You got by without reading the actual novels?" Something in her tone suggested that he'd admitted to being an ax murderer.

"I pulled Cs," he said. "There's nothing wrong with that."

She rolled her eyes. "There is when you could have read the books and gotten As or Bs. It's a form of cheating."

"No, it isn't. Besides, I read the CliffsNotes cover to cover."

"You missed out on a lot of great stories you wouldn't have normally read, so you cheated yourself."

He chuffed. "What do you want me to do? Confess to Miss Heinrich so I don't have to face a lifetime of guilt?"

He'd meant the comment to be snide, but the fact was, the guilt he actually carried wasn't likely to ease. And the reason it wouldn't had nothing to do with the hell he used to raise in school or the shortcuts he'd taken in the classes he hadn't liked.

"Well, at least you're reading it now." Tori returned to the task of setting out the plates of food—God only knew what the cook had thrown together tonight. Then she set out glasses of iced tea, silverware and napkins.

"What's for dinner?" he asked.

"It's a chicken and rice casserole."

"You could have fooled me."

Those hands, lightly freckled and neatly manicured, returned to her hips, and she gave him the eagle eye, much like Miss Heinrich used to do whenever it was her turn to watch over the detention room.

"Have you always been a jerk?" Tori asked. "Or is your surly tongue a result of the accident?"

The fact that she'd called him on his attitude didn't sit well with him, especially since he had little excuse. Well, actually, he figured he had a damn good one, but he wasn't about to spill his guts to her.

Besides, she ought to choose her battles.

"You're not the cook," he said, "so why are you getting so riled up?"

"Actually, Connie wasn't feeling well, and I volunteered to fix dinner tonight. So before you complain, you might take a bite."

"I never have cared much for casseroles."

"Do you like chicken?" she asked.

"Yes. If it's fried or barbecued."

"How about rice?"

He shrugged. "It's okay."

"Then give this a try."

"I like seeing the chicken and rice in two separate piles on my plate."

"I'll have to keep that in mind for the future." The spunky redhead got behind his wheelchair and pushed him to the desk, where she'd set a place for each of them.

Matt grumbled a complaint, but he picked up a fork anyway.

"You're acting like a spoiled baby. Maybe I ought to put a bib on you."

He shot her a warning glance. "Try it and you'll be sorry you got within arm's reach." If he got his hands on her—figuratively speaking, of course—he'd…he'd…

Damn. His mind took an unwelcome detour, and the thunder in his surly, empty threat suspended in midair.

Their gazes met and locked.

Sexual awareness, in all its heat and glory, flared, stirring up something more powerful than words. Something that, in spite of all his bluster, all his pain, was vibrant and medicinal, making him forget the shackles of guilt he hadn't been able to shake.

For a moment he almost felt whole again—as if that accident had never happened.

He wondered if it was because Tori reminded him of Cindy, but he quickly tossed that thought aside.

It was true there were similarities—the red hair, green eyes and fair complexion, not to mention that they were both nurturers, warm and loving to a fault.

Yet at this very moment, it was their differences that intrigued him, those things that set Tori apart and made her unique.

She was about six inches shorter than Cindy had been. And she wasn't anywhere near as easygoing and agreeable. She also had a hell of a stubborn streak.

Why else would she continue to stick around Matt when he'd done his best to run her off?

Unable to let his mind wander into forbidden territory, he broke eye contact and studied his plate, which was filled with a hearty helping of chicken and rice casserole, almond-dotted green beans and a golden-brown roll with slab of real butter.

Rather than lift his head and risk meeting her gaze again, he dug in.

To be honest, the casserole wasn't half-bad.

He knew he ought to say something, to thank her or praise the taste, but he'd be damned if he would allow himself to admit it. He didn't want her to get the wrong idea and think that they were actually creating some kind of friendship or bond.

She must have gotten the message, because they ate in silence until he'd cleaned his plate, which should've been proof enough that this dinner had been better than any Connie had made in the past couple of weeks. As far as meals went, Connie hadn't come up with anything to shout about, other than her desserts. Still, the casserole was better than mediocre and a part of him felt pressured to comment.

"Well," Tori said, pushing back the desk chair she'd been using and getting to her feet. "I told Connie I'd clean up the kitchen, too. And I need to feed the babies. They're probably hungry."

He hoped she didn't ask him for help with the kittens again. If she did, he'd have to tell her no.

Tori had him growing softer by the minute, and he couldn't afford to let down his defenses. She was too much like Cindy in all the wrong ways.

Too attractive.

Too appealing.

And when it came to Cindy, Matt had reason to believe that he'd gotten right and wrong mixed up.

Chapter Three

No one could ever accuse Matt of being obedient or backing down from a challenge.

So even though the orthopedic surgeon hadn't exactly given him the green light to get out of the wheelchair, he'd decided to take a shower after dinner anyway.

He'd gotten so sick and tired of those god-awful sponge baths that he'd been more than ready for the real thing. But that didn't mean he was stupid. He'd taken it slow and easy. And he would have quit the moment he'd had any reason to believe he was doing any permanent damage.

Still, standing had hurt like hell, and he'd been pretty shaky on his feet.

A couple of times he nearly slipped and fell, which could have been a real disaster, but he figured the doctor wouldn't have prescribed physical therapy if it wasn't time to stretch his legs.

Of course, he hadn't actually started the therapy yet.

A couple of weeks ago, when Jared had wheeled him into the clinic and was signing him in, Matt had noticed a wall in the waiting room that displayed photographs of all the therapists. While looking them over, he'd recognized Cindy's cousin, Joanne. The two young women had been raised next door to each other and were closer than most sisters.

Matt hadn't known which therapist would be assigned to work with him, but there was no way he'd risk running into the young woman who was undoubtedly still grieving Cindy's loss—and blaming Matt for it.

The last time he'd seen Joanne had been the day of the accident. Matt had gone with Cindy and her son to a Wilson family reunion at the city park. It would have been a tolerable day—and maybe even pleasant—if his competitive nature hadn't blown sky-high.

Cindy's ex-husband, another bronc rider Matt had met on the circuit, had shown up at the park. Dave had been an old neighbor of the Wilsons' and a friend of Cindy's brother, so it wasn't surprising that he would stop by. But things had grown more and more…awkward, not to mention competitive, as the day wore on.

After a while, Cindy had gotten angry at Matt, insisting that they leave before the day was over.

Matt suspected that, even if the accident hadn't happened on the way home, he would have wanted to avoid Joanne. There were several other occasions when Matt had sensed that Joanne was hoping and maybe even encouraging Cindy and Dave to reconcile, even though their divorce had been final before Matt had even entered the picture.

Joanne had given Cindy a goodbye hug, then she'd shot a frown at Matt, letting him know she thought he'd been out of line.

Matt hadn't thought so then.

But after the crash?

Well, there weren't any excuses that he could make—in public or in private—that would make him feel better about what he'd done. None that would hold water anyway.

So there was no way he was going to take a chance on seeing Joanne each time he went to the clinic.

"Let's get out of here," Matt had told his brother.

When Jared had tried to get him to see reason, Matt had reached up and gripped Jared's arm. "I'm not staying. And if you don't want to be embarrassed by my actions, you'll get me the hell out of here. *Now.*"

Apparently, Jared had figured out that Matt meant business, because he'd told the receptionist they'd have to reschedule. Then he opened the office door for Matt, who'd wheeled himself straight to the elevator.

When quizzed on the way back to Jared's ranch, Matt had told his brother he wasn't ready for therapy yet and refused to discuss what was really bothering him. Some things were too painful to talk about, even with family.

Then afterward, each time Jared had badgered him about it, Matt had merely clammed up.

Talking about it would only make it worse. Besides, what could Jared do to make it better?

Not one damn thing.

Now, as Matt wheeled himself out of his private bathroom and toward the bed, he was glad he'd taken the chance and showered this evening. The pounding water on his face and back had felt good, and so had his head after a good scrub with the shampoo. He managed to dry off and slip on a pair of shorts before his legs gave out.

He was thinking long and hard about turning in for the night when a knock sounded at the door.

"Who is it?" he asked, still not wanting to mix or mingle.

"It's Tori."

What now?

Earlier, the pretty redhead had seemed almost as eager to end the meal they'd shared as he'd been. But he sensed something in her voice. Something troubled.

"Come on in," he said.

She entered the door with a towel-wrapped kitten in her arms and concern etched across her brow. In fact, she seemed so worried that she'd obviously failed to realize she was wearing only a nightgown.

Or maybe she didn't think he'd notice, or that he wouldn't speculate she had on very little—if anything— underneath it.

"There's something wrong with Tippy," she said. "And I'm not sure what to do."

Matt had expected the cat to weaken. "He's the runt, Tori. And that means he's got two strikes against him already."

"What do you suggest we do? I don't want him to die."

Matt ought to focus on the cat, but he couldn't help studying Tori, who wore her wild Irish curls hanging loose and free, hair he could envision splayed against a pillowcase.

His pillowcase.

That white cotton gown she had on was the kind a grandma might wear, yet it took on a whole new look on Tori. He shouldn't find it the least bit sexy, but he did.

And so did his hormones, which were whooshing and pumping to life, letting him know that some of the long-forgotten parts of his body were still in their prime, his libido one of them.

Still, he tried to be sensitive to her concerns—a first for him in a long time. "Why don't you look for an eye-dropper. Maybe we can force some milk down him."

There he went again. Throwing out words like *we* and implying some kind of bond when there wasn't one. When there *shouldn't* be.

"Will you hold him while I go and look for one?" she asked, handing the kitten to him.

In spite of his reluctance to get involved, he took it from her.

How the hell was he supposed to tell her no?

After she left the room, he looked the runt over carefully. It seemed perfectly formed, just smaller than the rest. But it was definitely weaker.

If Tippy didn't pull through, and that was becoming more and more possible, he sensed that Tori was going to take it hard. The orphaned critters had become more than barn cats to her, and she seemed to have bonded with each one of them.

Early on, he'd learned to stay detached, which wasn't always easy to do. But a guy sure didn't have to make friends with the four-legged creatures that lived on a ranch or farm. Losing a pet was tough on some people.

That's why Matt never named animals.

Not anymore.

Tori, of course, wasn't of that same mind-set. She'd named each of the kittens, and if truth be told, he figured she was trying to get him to feel that same affection, which he was doing his best to fight.

But he'd even begun to think of the baby cats as Pumpkin, Fur Ball and Boswell. Since neither of the two solid-black kittens in the litter had any markings to distinguish them, it was impossible for him to tell them apart. But Tori seemed to have an innate sense of which one was Stormy and which was Midnight.

"I'm back." She swept into the room, the hem of her gown several inches above her ankles, revealing bare feet.

His gaze traveled from her pretty, cotton-candy-pink toenails to her head. He had to force himself to glance away from her face so that he could look at the bottle full of formula and the eyedropper she was showing him.

"I hope this does the trick," she said.

Well, it certainly could. But there were no guarantees, and he hated to be the one to tell her. Instead he watched her unscrew the top, dip the dropper into the bottle and squeeze the bulb to draw in the milk.

"Okay," she said. "You hold open his mouth, and I'll try to get this down him."

She stood close enough for Matt to catch a hint of her shampoo, something floral. Lilac, maybe? He took another whiff, relishing the scent of woman.

As she stooped over the kitten, the neckline of her

cotton nightgown gaped open, revealing the swell of a perfectly formed breast and the dusky edge of a nipple.

Damn.

"Be careful," she said. "Help me hold his head still."

It wasn't the kitten his hands itched to hold, to touch, to stroke and caress…

She moved to the right, trying to get the dropper into Tippy's mouth, but all Matt could seem to do was watch the scooped neckline swoosh this way and that and catch another glimpse of her breasts, soft and full and begging for a man's hand.

Double damn.

Uncomfortable with the way his thoughts were going, he tried his best to focus on Tippy. Hopefully, the runt would perk up soon.

If this joint feeding venture was dragged out much longer, Matt wasn't sure how much of this his libido could stand.

Still, as her arm brushed his shoulder, jolting him with simmering heat, the scent of lilacs mingled with her peppermint-fresh breath, taunting him.

Did she have any idea what she and her ready-for-bed appearance were doing to him?

Tori studied the eyedropper, wondering how much Tippy had eaten. He was just a little guy, so she didn't want to over-feed him. But she wanted to make sure he got enough, too.

Straightening from where she'd been bent over Matt's lap, she said, "That's probably enough for now, but I'm going to set the alarm every hour and feed him through the night."

She arched and stretched, hoping to work out a kink in her back. As she turned toward Matt, she saw that his eyes were on her and not the kitten.

But he wasn't merely watching her.

There was an intensity in his gaze that nearly took her breath away, jolting her with sexual awareness.

She'd been so worried about Tippy that she'd forgotten she was only wearing a nightgown.

Feeling as unbalanced and self-conscious as a woman who'd just woken up in a window display at a bustling department store, she crossed her arms over her breasts. "I, uh, guess I should have put on a robe."

"No problem." His blue eyes glimmered, male interest burning bright.

He glanced at the lamp that glowed behind her, and she suddenly realized the light had made her gown almost useless.

She shifted her weight to one hip. "You should have said something."

"And lose the best view I've had in ages?" His mouth quirked at one side, and humor glimmered in his eyes.

It pleased her that he found her attractive, in spite of the fact that she ought to be uneasy about that.

But Matt Clayton was one heck of a handsome man.

She could almost imagine him swaggering across the ranch or riding a bucking bronco, one hand on the saddle horn and the other in the air, as the crowd roared their approval.

Yet even sitting here in a wheelchair, his hair damp and mussed, he was breathtakingly male.

His scent, which she'd failed to recognize earlier, was

clean and brisk, a pleasant blend of soap and musk. And with each breath she took, her pulse kicked up a notch.

He hadn't shaved in a while, and the light stubble of his beard gave him a rugged appearance she found far more appealing than she should.

"I'd better take Tippy back to his brothers and sisters," she said, reaching for the kitten.

Matt snagged one of her corkscrew curls, gently pulling it straight, then letting it go. "Is it natural?"

"The curl?" she asked. "Or the color?"

His gaze dropped to her hips, as though he expected the lamplight shining through the cotton material to provide him further proof.

She ought to be annoyed.

Yet instead, she felt a bit naughty and more of a flirt than ever before. "The kids used to call me Strawberry Short-cake when I was a girl. So does that answer your question?"

"For now."

His words and the implication that he'd want further proof someday caused her pulse to first spike, then skitter through her veins, a heated reaction she hadn't expected.

She tried to remind herself that Matthew was her employer's son. And that, while she could no longer be a nurse, she ought to consider him as off-limits as any other patient.

Besides, she didn't need to get involved with anyone right now, especially one with all the baggage she suspected Matt carried. After all, she'd moved from Dallas to Brighton Valley to get away from her own memories, so why take on someone else's?

Still, she suspected that it was good for Matthew to see

himself as a sexual being again. It just might help him to heal, to forget about the past and to move on with his life. And the dedicated nurse who still lived inside of her, the professional who'd once loved her career more than anything in this world, insisted that encouraging Matt to move beyond his pain was a good thing.

But on the other hand, the heated physical response she'd had to his innuendos and the desire simmering in his eyes only served to remind her how long it had been since she'd felt any sexual longing. So she decided the wisest thing for her to do tonight was to excuse herself and get out of the line of fire and temptation.

"Thanks for helping me feed Tippy," she said.

He didn't respond.

Neither did he try to stop her from turning around and walking away, ending things before they had a chance to start.

Early the next morning Matt sequestered himself in the office, a dark-paneled room that was located in the house, just a couple of doors down the hall from his old bedroom.

He had plenty of reasons to hide away from distractions, and Tori was definitely one of them.

Last night, while she'd been in his room, he'd been bombarded with thoughts and desires he'd never expected to experience again.

And he wasn't sure how he felt about that.

His hormones were willing, but common sense urged him to beware.

All during the night he'd heard her alarm go off and knew she was taking care of the kittens, which now resided in her bedroom. But she didn't ask for his help any of those times, and he was grateful for that.

Between the taunting glimpses of her breasts and the desire to get a clearer view of what lay hidden beneath her white cotton gown, he was going to have a hard time keeping his hands and his thoughts to himself.

Still, he couldn't help wondering why she hadn't come looking for him yet.

He glanced at the clock. It was nearly noon. Had she been avoiding him, too?

Probably.

Evading her had been his own game plan, which was why he was in the office.

Sure, he'd agreed to hold down the fort for Sabrina, the bookkeeper, while she was at Jared's ranch helping little Joey recover from surgery. But that had nothing to do with Matt closing the door and demanding privacy this morning when the room was usually open to anyone passing in the hall.

Actually, it had been a good idea to shut himself inside. Without any interruptions, he'd gotten a lot of work done so far.

He'd gone over the books, noting that Sabrina had everything in order. He'd also reconciled the latest bank statement, which hadn't balanced at first. But it hadn't taken him long to figure out why, and he soon had it all squared away.

Next he planned to pay the monthly bills, which he'd pulled from the to-be-paid file and placed in a stack.

Several of the statements had sticky notes on top, which Sabrina had left to remind herself—or in this case,

Matt, who was her temporary replacement—to call and have the companies fax the missing invoices. One he'd gotten that chore taken care of, he studied the to-do list Tori had given him for Granny's party. He'd better check out the prices and availability of portable potties and the damn buckboard she insisted they needed.

He thumbed through the yellow pages in the phone book, then chose a couple of companies he knew were reputable.

As he picked up the telephone to dial the first number, footsteps, heavier than usual, sounded in the hall. They paused before the door, then a soft knock sounded.

Matt looked up from his work. "Yes?"

"It's me," a gravelly, male voice said. "Can I come in?"

The man didn't identify himself, but he didn't need to. It was Lester, the ranch foreman.

"Sure." Matt watched the door swing open and the rangy, fifty-something cowboy walk in.

"I was in town picking up supplies," Lester said, "so I stopped at the post office to get the mail."

"Thanks. I appreciate that."

"Here you go." Lester dropped a stack on the desk. "It's mostly bills, I suspect."

Matt scanned the top envelope, noting the logo of the phone company.

"So how are those kittens doing?" Lester asked.

"I haven't heard Tori crying, so I figure they're still alive."

"That gal sure is a softie," Lester said. "Reminds me of my sister, Irene. She never did see a sick or injured critter she didn't want to nurse back to health."

"There's a runt that isn't doing too well," Matt said. "And, wouldn't you know, that's the one Tori took a liking to."

"That sounds a lot like my sister," Lester said. "Once, when Irene was just a kid, she found two orphaned baby sparrows and brought them home, nest and all. She kept them alive for a day or two, but they both died. And she damn near fell apart. I didn't think she was ever going to stop bawling."

That's what Matt was afraid of. Tori was setting herself up for heartache.

"Well," Lester said, "I'd better get back to work. Hank told me there's a large section of fence that needs to be replaced in the south pasture. I thought I'd better go check it out."

Matt nodded, wishing he could ride with the men and do some good, hard labor. To feel the sun beating on his face and the perspiration gathering on his brow. Sitting in this damn chair was getting old fast.

Lester shut the door behind him, leaving Matt to the phone calls he'd needed to make.

Twenty minutes later he was going to take a break from writing out the checks to pay the monthly bills and head to the kitchen for lunch. But having second thoughts, he decided to wait until everyone else had already eaten.

Okay, so he was still hoping to avoid Tori.

He took the stack of mail Lester had brought, thumbed through it and tossed out the fliers and junk. He made a pile of anything that would interest Granny or that needed her attention, like a newsletter from the Brighton Valley Community Church and a save-the-date notice from the Ladies Aid Society. But when his eyes landed on an envelope addressed to Tori, his interest piqued.

Odd, he thought, as he noted the return address: Sean McKenzie.

Tori's last name was McKenzie, wasn't it?

So who was this guy?

A brother?

A husband?

Under his name, he'd written: In care of Twin Oaks Ranch. Matt had heard about that place before. He'd been roped into helping with a charity event, and the proceeds went there. It was a rehab place of some kind.

Curiosity damn near threatened to burn a hole in Matt's brain.

Apparently, the woman who'd been dead set on prying into his misery and his past had a few secrets of her own. And Matt was determined to learn what they were.

What would it hurt?

Worst case scenario, she'd get mad at him for prying. But what was so bad about that? It might make her back off and leave him alone.

And if it didn't?

Maybe it would toss a bucket of cold water on whatever had been zapping and buzzing between them last night.

Chapter Four

The oldest of three children, Tori supposed it had only been natural for her to fall into the role of a nurturer and to grow up responsible. And that was also one of the reasons she'd chosen to get a degree in nursing.

It had been a perfect career.

As she sprayed window cleaner onto the glass door of the china hutch in the formal dining room at the Rocking C Ranch, she blew out a sigh. Yes, it did seem a little odd to be employed as a maid now.

But it wasn't as though she minded the work.

Over the years she'd taken on a lot of the chores, like cooking and scrubbing and chasing after her younger brother and sister. So she knew what was expected of her.

Not that she'd be working at the Rocking C forever. She'd go back to being a nurse again someday.

She unrolled a length of paper towels from the roll and climbed onto the stepstool so she could reach the top of the glass panels on the door.

No, having a job as a maid hadn't been part of the game plan, but the pay was okay, and Granny provided her room and board. The best part of it all was being able to put plenty of distance between herself, her self-centered siblings and the problems and heartbreak they'd caused her.

As she wiped down the glass until it shined, she heard footsteps as someone sauntered across the hardwood floor. She looked up and watched Lester make his way through the living room and enter the hall with a stack of mail in his hands.

If he had noticed her, she would have acknowledged him or said hello. But he walked with a determined step, intent upon where he was going.

At the office door, he rapped lightly, which caused her to pause and wait to see if he'd be invited in.

The office door had been closed for most of the morning, so she'd assumed Matthew had wanted some privacy and had decided to clean that particular room last. She'd just been waiting for him to come out.

In the meantime, she'd been focusing her attention on some of the special projects she'd planned to do today, such as dusting the bookshelf in the living room, wiping down the shutters and cleaning out the handcrafted oak hutch in the dining room.

Within moments Lester came out of the office, his arms now empty. As he strode out of the house, she wondered what Matthew was doing inside.

Bookwork, she supposed, but whenever Sabrina had

gone over the accounts or paid bills, the door had always remained open.

She knew Matt was struggling with depression after his accident, something Jared had been worried about. So it concerned her whenever he was holed up by himself.

For that reason she climbed down from the stepstool, left her cleaning supplies near the hutch and went to check on him.

As she stood before the door, she knocked lightly.

"What is it?" he asked.

Neither his response nor the snippy tone had been an invitation to enter, but she opted to take it as such and let herself in.

Matt was sitting at the desk, where he'd pushed the tufted leather seat aside to make room for the wheelchair. He appeared busy; there were some files and stacks of paper on the desktop.

But her interest was drawn to the man himself.

He'd showered this morning; she'd known because she'd cleaned his bathroom already. But he hadn't combed his golden-wheat-colored hair. Or maybe he had, but he'd run his fingers through the strands numerous times throughout the morning.

His square-cut jaw seemed to shout defiance, as did the fact that he still hadn't shaved. The light bristle on his cheeks gave him a dark and edgy aura, which appealed to her more than it should have.

His eyes, the color of a field of Texas bluebonnets, provided him with a softness he might not fully appreciate. And when his gaze locked on her, it darn near turned her stomach inside out.

She tucked a loose strand of her hair behind her ear, inadvertently catching a whiff of ammonia from the cleaning product she'd been using, which only served to remind her of her place. She was, after all, just an employee who had no right to gawk at her boss's son.

Yet the sight of Matt stirred something deep inside of her. Something profoundly female and sexual.

She tried to shake off her interest, her momentary attraction, but she probably hadn't been very good at doing so, because Matt leaned back in his wheelchair and crossed his arms, then asked, "Can I help you?"

"I, uh…" Great. Now she was at a loss for words, which rarely happened to her.

Think, Tori. Think.

She cleared her throat. "I was wondering when this room would be available for me to clean."

"It's a big house. Surely you can find somewhere else to be."

"Yes, I suppose I can." Still, her legs didn't move. And neither did her gaze, her perusal of the man.

Even in that chair, Matthew Clayton had a commanding presence.

"Who's Sean McKenzie?" he asked, completely drawing her out of her girlish musing.

Her heart thumped in her chest, and her lips parted. "Why do you want to know?"

He held up a letter addressed to her, in care of the ranch.

She recognized her brother's handwriting and stiffened. Her first thought was to question how Sean would have known where to find her. Then she realized her grandmother must have given him her contact information.

For a moment she wished she hadn't let Gram know where she was, but she couldn't have done that. Someone in the family had to be responsible. And Lord knew the elderly woman couldn't depend upon the other two siblings, the kids who had been coddled until they'd become self-centered and spoiled rotten—and damaged in their own way.

Matt placed the letter on the desktop and pushed it across the polished oak toward Tori.

Her first impulse was to open the envelope and make sure that her grandmother was okay, that an emergency hadn't arisen. But that was good ol' dependable Tori's natural response. And she was determined not to enable the younger McKenzies any more.

No, if his attempt to contact her had anything to do with her grandmother, her brother would have called, not written a letter.

So she took the envelope and slowly tore it up in pieces. Then she stashed the remnants in the pocket of her apron.

Matt watched her carefully, one of his brows arched and indicating surprise or maybe confusion.

"Sean McKenzie is my brother," she said.

Then before he could question her further, before she felt compelled to vent, she turned and walked away, leaving him to stew in his curiosity.

Connie served meat loaf for dinner that night, but by the time Matt got a chance to sit at the table, he'd learned that the ranch hands who'd eaten earlier had used up all the ketchup.

He couldn't fault them for that, he supposed, since

they'd undoubtedly tried to do what he was hoping to do—mask the flavor of baked hamburger that tasted more like cardboard than meat.

Still, he swore under his breath and reached for the bowl that held the potatoes, which didn't look too bad— what was left of them anyway.

Fortunately, there was still a lemon meringue pie left, but only because Connie had hidden it from the hands, who'd eaten earlier. He'd bet that they'd left plenty of meat loaf, though.

How in the hell Connie could make such lousy meals, yet whip up great cakes and cookies, was beyond him.

At least it hadn't taken the new cook very long to realize she had to double and triple her dessert recipes so she didn't have a dinnertime rebellion on her hands.

If she were smart, she'd ask Tori to trade jobs with her more often. That chicken and rice casserole had been one of the best dinners they'd had in a long time. But Matt figured Tori had enough to do around here without taking on more work.

He glanced to his right, where the redhead sat, picking at the food on her plate.

Granny was across the table from him. He could have sworn he'd seen the elderly woman grimace as she choked down her meal. Yet she never said a word to Connie, other than, "Thanks for dinner."

Matt was still hungry, but pushed his plate aside. If he'd been more mobile, he might have helped clear the table. But the damn wheelchair was bulky and difficult enough to move through the house.

He glanced at Tori, watched her scrape the meringue off the top of her pie and dig into the lemon filling.

What was her story?

How had she come to wind up on the ranch?

When he'd finished his second helping of pie, he asked if she wanted to take a walk outside with him this evening. No need to quiz her in front of Granny, which might only make things more awkward than necessary.

She looked up from her plate. "You want to go for a walk? With *me?*"

"Well, you'd be doing the walking," he said. "I'd have to wheel around in this thing."

She bit her bottom lip. What made the question so difficult? Had he been so tough on her that she had to decide whether or not she wanted to be alone with him?

Or was she thinking about the sexual attraction that had ricocheted throughout the office earlier?

Damn. It wasn't as though he was going to make any moves on her. Matt didn't start something he couldn't finish.

Of course, it wasn't as though he *couldn't* finish something with her. In that sense, the wheelchair was just a bit of an inconvenience. If they were stretched out on a bed, he'd...

Hell, he'd put a sated smile on both of their faces.

"Sure," Tori said. "I'd like to take a walk."

"That's a very good idea." Granny pushed her chair back and got to her feet. "You two go on outside while I help Connie with the dishes."

Matt hoped Granny wasn't thinking that he and Tori were tiptoeing around a romance. He knew better than to get involved with anyone again, especially another redhead—and a bossy one at that. But there'd been several questions weighing on his mind.

Questions that demanded answers. Like why she was no longer a nurse. Why she'd shut her brother out of her life.

Matt wouldn't be living at the Rocking C forever. Eventually, he'd heal and get on with his own life—even if he didn't have a clue what he'd do with the rest of it, now that he couldn't be a rodeo cowboy anymore.

Either way, when he decided to ride off into the sunset, he was going to have to feel good about leaving Granny with a cook who didn't know her way around a stove and a woman who'd rather be a maid than utilize a nursing degree.

Something just didn't add up.

Matt maneuvered his wheelchair away from the table, then rolled into the kitchen and out to the service porch, where Tori opened the door for him. As he started down the ramp, she reached for the handles at his back.

"I've got it," he said. Hell, the last time she tried to help, he'd been afraid the chair would barrel down that ramp like a wild bronc out of the chute.

Moments later, when he'd reached the ground safely on his own, she joined him in the yard.

"Where to?" she asked.

He nodded toward the barn, then began to push the wheels of his chair forward.

"I'm afraid I ate more pie than I should have, so it's nice to get outside and walk off some of the calories."

Matt couldn't care less about fresh air and exercise, but he wanted to get her alone. So most any direction would do. "Let's walk along the driveway. That outdoor light at the back of the barn ought to illuminate our way for a while."

"All right." She scanned the horizon. "It's a pretty night."

"Yep." He glanced at the evening sky, where a lovers' moon shone bright, and a jillion tiny stars winked as though they were in on some kind of celestial secret.

As they walked and wheeled along, the sounds and the smells of the ranch soon lulled Matt into an easy mood.

Had it done the same to her?

There was a stretch of pasture to the left, as well as to the right. He remembered the first day the social worker had driven him along this very road and told him she'd found him a new home.

He'd been scared and angry, yet he'd been in awe of the place, too. It was a lot different from the city streets or the small apartment in which he'd lived with his uncle.

"I love this ranch," he said.

"It's easy to see why you would."

He supposed the Rocking C held a certain appeal to a lot of people, especially a boy. In Matt's case, it had been the vast grassy pastures and the animals that had roped his interest first. Then it had been the men who'd taken him under their wing, the self-satisfaction of a hard day in the saddle and the reward of a warm, cozy bed at night.

And before he knew it, he'd found the real key to contentment—a mother's love and a sense of belonging that had always eluded him.

He slid a glance at the pretty redhead who walked beside him. Would she feel better about sharing something personal with him if he opened up a bit first?

Maybe.

"Did Granny ever tell you how she and I first met?" he asked.

Tori slowed and turned, her face bathed in moonlight, interest sparking in her eyes. "No. But I'd like to hear about it."

"When I was about ten, I tried to steal her purse."

"No kidding?"

"Well, it's kind of a long story." He glanced over his shoulder at the house and nodded. "Let's head back before it gets too dark to see."

"Okay."

For a moment he questioned his plan to share the details with a virtual stranger. But then again, it wasn't anything that she couldn't find out by asking Granny.

So he turned the wheelchair around and began to tell Tori what he'd never told anyone. Not even Cindy, the woman he'd planned to marry. "I was a city boy by birth. And I lived in downtown Dallas with my mom until I was nine."

"What about your father?"

"He took off when I was just a baby, so I don't remember him."

"I'm sorry."

He shrugged. "It all worked out for the best, I guess."

Again he questioned the wisdom in spilling his guts, then realized he wasn't telling her any real secrets. "Since it was just us, my mom had to work two jobs to pay the rent, so I learned to fend for myself early on."

Matt had more or less been on his own since he'd been Joey's age. At the time, he hadn't seen anything unusual about it. There were a lot of kids in his neighborhood who'd learned the ropes while on the street.

"Were you close to your mom?" Tori asked.

"Yeah. I suppose so. But she died when I was nine."

"I'm sorry to hear that."

Matt had been, too. But not as sorry as he'd been after moving in with Uncle Vern. "A social worker called my mom's half brother, and when he agreed to take me, I moved to Brighton Valley."

"How did that go?" she asked. "I mean, you eventually moved to the ranch, so I figured it might not have worked out."

"It didn't. I guess you could say we butted heads more often than not. Vern didn't like anyone to cross him, and I wasn't used to having a boss."

"You argued a lot?"

"My uncle had this warped idea that he could beat or starve me into submission." Looking back, Matt supposed that had merely served to help him develop an even tougher hide and spirit.

Tori crossed her arms and shifted her weight to one leg. "That's barbaric."

"Unfortunately, that's also a reality for some kids." Matt raked a hand through his hair. "Anyway, one day, as I was wandering through town and making excuses not to go home, I came upon an ice cream social that was sponsored by the church. I hadn't eaten since the night before, and even then, it hadn't been much. So I was really hungry. I didn't have any money, and the only option I saw was to steal a lady's purse."

"Was it Granny's purse?" Tori asked.

"Yeah, but I didn't know who she was then. I just saw that she had gray hair and was kind of pudgy. So I figured she'd be no match for me in a foot race. But little did I know that Granny was just as tough and cagey as she was loving."

"What did she do?"

"She caught me before I could get ten yards away. And she knew right off the bat that I'd been neglected and mistreated—probably because I was so skinny and was sporting a bruised cheek and a split lip. So, after she bought me all the ice cream I could eat, she reported the abuse. And when authorities investigated my living situation and decided to remove me from my uncle's home, she offered me a place to live on the ranch."

"And you ended up becoming a part of her family."

"Eventually. But it was tough at first. One of the things I'd learned growing up was to protect myself by not caring, by withdrawing. It took her a while, but Granny drew me out of my shell. And before long, the men on the ranch began to show me the way adults ought to treat children."

"That's a nice ending to a sad story," she said.

"Yeah, I guess it is."

Tori studied the man in the wheelchair, appreciating his self-disclosure. Her heart had gone out to the little boy in him, the defiant child who, by Matt's own admission, had learned to protect himself by withdrawing, by pretending not to care about anyone or anything.

Apparently, as an adult, he'd fallen back into that same old pattern when tragedy struck.

She wanted to ask about the woman who'd died, the woman he'd loved. But she thought it was best to wait until it was his idea to tell her.

"Why don't we sit on the porch?" she asked.

"I'd have to park this thing and climb the steps. But that's okay. There's a railing."

"No, it's *not* okay." For some reason she'd completely

forgotten about his limitations, in spite of that darn wheel-chair. "I can't allow you to do something the doctor hasn't said you could do. And I'm sorry for being so thought-less as to even suggest it."

"If you want to sit outside," he said, "get yourself a chair from the porch and bring it here."

"All right." Tori made two trips back and forth, bringing first a wicker rocker, then a small matching side table that bore a ceramic pot holding a citronella candle.

"All we need is a match," she said before dashing into the house to get one.

Minutes later they sat outdoors, the flame flickering on the wick while a sliver of curly smoke snaked into the night sky, promising to fend off any insects that might be lurking nearby.

A horse whinnied in the distance, and crickets chirped near the water trough. It might not seem like a romantic setting to anyone else, but it did to Tori, and she found it surprisingly appealing.

She enjoyed the stillness for a while, the peace.

"So how did *you* meet Granny?" Matt asked, drawing her from her appreciation of the night.

"I was in Brighton Valley, filling out a job application at Caroline's Diner."

Tori didn't think she should mention that Granny, who'd been eating a muffin with a friend and sharing a cup of coffee, had spotted Tori crying her eyes out. If she did, he'd probably ask what had caused her tears. And, if she wanted to be honest, she'd have to admit that she'd realized the owner of the café wanted her to list her previous employers, as well as provide the names and contact numbers for any supervisors she'd had.

She could have lied on the application, she supposed, but dishonesty had always gone against her grain. And if a person didn't have any honor, what did they have left?

"Why did you decide to become a maid rather than a waitress?" he asked.

Actually, Tori would have preferred to be a *nurse*. It's what she'd been trained to do. It's what she loved.

But the betrayal and embarrassment were still so fresh, her feelings so raw, that she wasn't ready to explain herself or to discuss her brother's crime with a potential employer.

Of course, that hadn't seemed to matter when Granny sat beside her and offered a tissue. Moments later the story had just tumbled out, along with a new onslaught of tears. It had seemed a real blessing to have someone sympathize with her heartbreak and disappointment, to understand her need for some R & R.

"Your mother provided a maternal connection I'd been missing for a long time," Tori admitted. "And before I knew it, I began to bare my heart and soul to her, revealing things I'd never expected to tell anyone."

"So when she offered you a job, you took it because she was motherly?"

"I'm not trying to overstep my bounds," she said, hoping he understood. She wasn't attempting to worm her way into his family. "I really don't know why I came out to the Rocking C with her. Maybe because she was so kind. Maybe because she offered me room and board, too. Maybe because I wanted to..."

Be careful, she advised herself. Telling Granny had

been one thing. But sharing the same with Matt was out of the question. He didn't need to know that she'd wanted to get away from her family so she could regroup and become completely independent of them. So she side-stepped the fact altogether and added, "Well, because I wanted to spend some time in the country."

"You obviously know your way around a stove better than Connie," he said. "So why didn't you get her job?"

"Elsie Tuttle, the previous cook, hadn't retired yet, so Granny's only opening was for a housekeeper. And when Connie came along, Elsie had just announced that she was moving in with her daughter in Galveston, so that's the position she was offered."

"Did you ever think about swapping jobs with Connie?" Matt asked.

"Actually, yes. Connie hasn't had much experience as a cook, although she did work in a bakery for a while. But your mother wouldn't hear of it. And I'll be darned if I know why. Sometimes she almost flinches when she looks at some of the dishes Connie puts out on the table. And she usually takes double helpings of dessert, too—just like we all do. But I've never heard her complain."

"I'm afraid it's impossible to second-guess my mother and figure out what her real objective is," Matt said. "And even if some of her plans are far-fetched, her motives always come from the heart."

"Well, obviously, she has her reasons." Tori wasn't sure what they could possibly be, though.

"So why did you give up nursing?" Matt asked.

While she supposed it was natural for him to have posed that question, she pondered her response. The truth wasn't something she wanted to run up a flagpole for all the world to see.

She tucked a strand of hair behind her ear. "Let's just say that it seemed like the right thing to do at the time. I might go back. We'll see." Then she glanced out into the pasture, into the night. "Have you given any more thought to Granny's birthday party?"

If he suspected she was trying her best to avoid any more revelations about herself, he didn't mention it. Instead he said, "No, I haven't given it much thought at all."

"Why not? I'd think that you'd be excited about helping her celebrate."

"I'm happy that she's having a birthday. But the kind of party you're envisioning seems like an awfully big chore."

"It's *not* too much work." She glanced his way, saw him watching her intently, and her voice just naturally lowered, softened. "Not if we share the load."

"Why does this party mean so much to you?" he asked.

"Because Granny trusted me, a virtual stranger to her. And she provided me with a job and a place to live."

"Doc Graham has a lot of pull at the clinic in Wexler," Matt said. "I'd think that working with him would be a lot more fulfilling for you."

Maybe someday, she thought. But not yet. "I'm enjoying a break from nursing right now."

She thought she heard him scoff, but couldn't be sure. Still, she couldn't blame him for not believing her. She'd been in her element whenever one of the hands was injured. Why, just a couple of weeks ago, when Charlie McDougall suffered a gash in his head and refused to see a doctor, she'd actually gotten a lot of satisfaction out of convincing him otherwise. And in spite of her fears for Joey's health, she'd received a rush of personal fulfillment when she'd been able to detect the seriousness of his heart condition and had accompanied him to the hospital for the tests and subsequent surgery.

No, she might be enjoying the break from her younger siblings. But she didn't like being away from nursing.

Was Matt buying into her lie?

She was afraid to steal a glance his way. Instead she gazed at the full moon and the vast array of stars, her mood growing solemn, pensive.

Matt spun his chair a few degrees to the right, facing her full on. "Can I ask you something?"

Her heart skipped a beat, and for a moment she wondered if he was turning the conversation toward something…personal. Something romantic. And she wasn't sure if she'd be flattered or uneasy.

"Sure," she told him. "Ask away."

"Why did you tear up your brother's letter without reading it?"

So much for him leaning toward romance, which would have put her on the spot—whether she was flattered by the idea or not. But the question about her brother took her completely aback.

She slapped at a mosquito that lit on her arm. "I'd rather not discuss it."

"Fair enough." His gaze traveled to the pasture, where a couple of the brood mares grazed.

"Now I have a question for *you*," Tori said.

"I guess turnabout is fair play. Shoot."

"Jared told me that you quit physical therapy. Why? Don't you care whether you walk again or not?"

Matt continued to stare off into distance for a while, as if he hadn't heard her. Or, if he had, that he wasn't sure he wanted to discuss his thoughts or reasons with her.

When she suspected he wasn't going to give her an answer at all, he surprised her. "The first time Jared drove me to physical therapy, I realized that there was someone who worked there that I didn't want to run into. So I refused to take my appointment."

"And so, for some crazy reason, you'd rather risk the chance of not having a full recovery from your injury."

"First of all, the reason wasn't crazy. And second, I'll never be one hundred percent. Not as long as I can't ever ride in another rodeo. So what the hell difference does it make?"

It ought to make a lot of difference, and she struggled to figure out what was really going on in that head of his.

"Who were you trying to avoid?" she asked.

"No one important."

"Was it a woman?" she asked.

"Yeah, but not for the reason you're thinking."

Oh, no? She suspected that the woman had been an old lover. And that their breakup had been messy. Yet something told her that even if she was partially right, there was more to it than that.

"I'll probably have physical therapy someday," he added, "but it'll have to be at another place."

Good. At least they were making progress.

"You mean you'd consider making an appointment in Brighton Valley?"

"Sure, but it's a pretty small town. I doubt if there's a physical therapist there."

Tori studied the man who didn't seem to be in any hurry to walk again.

As a rodeo cowboy, competition had undoubtedly come easy for him. So it seemed reasonable to believe that he'd want to do all he could to get back on his feet.

"If I find another place and drive you back and forth, will you go?" she asked.

Matt hesitated, but only for a moment. "I'll think about it."

Good. She'd love to give something back to Granny. And she couldn't think of anything better than a healthier son who would soon get out of that wheelchair and quit feeling sorry for himself.

Still, something niggled at her. A whittling sense of guilt that chipped away at her self-confidence.

And why was that?

Because, a small voice whispered, *in some respects, when it comes to not giving one hundred percent, Matt isn't that different from you.*

Chapter Five

While Tori enjoyed the time she'd spent outdoors with Matt this evening, she hadn't been able to shake a subtle sense of guilt for not practicing what she intended to preach.

She wanted Matt to push himself, yet she was content to sit back and not be the woman she was meant to be.

"But in my case," she argued to herself, "it's a different story."

She was just taking a little breather, a little time off to regain her balance. Besides, there always seemed to be some kind of medical emergency on the ranch, giving her plenty of opportunities to be a nurse while not actually working at a hospital or clinic.

To be honest, though, Tori missed her job in a busy E.R. and having the opportunity to sharpen her medical skills.

However, life on the Rocking C was slow paced, which made it a perfect place for her to heal her own wounds.

Now, as she sat in the guest bedroom that she'd been assigned to use, the muted sounds of Matt's television hummed from the room next door. But she ignored it, instead focusing on what had persuaded her to escape her family in the first place.

As much as she loved her maternal grandparents, she wished they hadn't coddled her younger brother and sister and spoiled them rotten.

Deep inside, Tori knew the elderly couple hadn't meant to cause Sean and Jenna any harm. They'd only tried to make up for the devastating loss of their parents.

But while growing up as orphans was a tough row to hoe, it was, unfortunately, their reality and something they had to learn to deal with.

It would have been better if Gram and Gramps had been loving yet firm. If they had, Sean and Jenna might have grown up stronger and more grounded—at least morally and ethically.

Tori had been in high school when her parents had taken a second honeymoon and died in a fluke helicopter accident on the trip. She'd been devastated, too, but at least her character had already been molded.

So after graduating, she went off to college and eventually became a registered nurse.

Her life had really looked promising and bright.

Then, after Sean had a falling out with some of his loser friends, Gram called and asked Tori if he could move in with her. She agreed, hoping that he'd finally grown up. She got him a job at the hospital, and before long, Jenna came looking for help, too. Soon there were three McKenzies working at Lone Star General.

Okay, so the living and working situation had required an adjustment, but she'd felt good about helping out her brother and sister.

That is, until a significant amount of prescription pain medication turned up missing from the hospital.

Tori had never expected one of the thieves to be her brother.

A criminal investigation uncovered his stash, and Tori had been mortified. His defense attorney managed to get him minimal jail time, a fine and probation. Then, as if the shame hadn't been enough, Tori had been reprimanded by the hospital for her lack of judgment in referring her brother and for missing all the signs of his drug addiction.

Just when she thought things couldn't possibly get worse, she found her sister lip-locked with Dr. James Dawson in one of the supply closets at the hospital. James, an intern at Lone Star General, also happened to be the man Tori was dating. The man who was her first—and only—lover.

Needless to say, Tori was crushed to learn that James wasn't the man she'd hoped he was—that he was a womanizer and couldn't be trusted.

But Jenna was her *sister*. And even though Jenna had only been eighteen and was still a babe in many ways, some kind of sisterly code of honor should have been at play. And it hadn't been.

Feeling betrayed and even more embarrassed than ever, Tori quit her job, broke the lease on her apartment and moved out of town.

All she wanted to do was put some distance between herself and the past. So she'd ended up in Brighton Valley, looking for work and a place to rent. She'd begun to run out of hope and funds when she met Granny Clayton. And that's when her luck finally turned.

Or had it?

Could she ever really escape from the past, the embarrassment or the heartbreak?

Maybe she ought to make that separation from her family permanent.

The guilt that had been hovering over her since talking to Matt about putting out a hundred percent stretched over her like a new rubber band, ready to snap and sting.

She might not want to ever see her brother and sister again, but Gram was another story.

Gramps had died last year—before the family had begun to unravel—and now Gram was alone. No matter how you looked at it, Tori was the only person upon whom the elderly woman could depend.

So, no. While Gram was alive, Tori could never fully sever herself from her siblings.

She reached for her purse, pulled out her cell and dialed Gram's number.

Unfortunately, Jenna answered on the second ring.

Tori's first impulse was to ask, "Have you met any new interns lately? Have you set your sights on someone else's lover?"

Instead she merely asked to speak to Gram.

"You have no idea how sorry I am," Jenna said. "About everything."

Tori tensed. Her little sister had been so used to having

her way that she hadn't cared what effect her choices or her behavior might have on someone else. And quite frankly, there was no reason to even go there; what was done, was done.

"May I please speak to Gram?" Tori asked again.

"Yes. But can you wait a minute? I wanted to tell you that, if it makes you feel better, James and I aren't seeing each other anymore."

"It would have made me *feel* better if you hadn't considered him fair game in the first place."

"I know, but—"

"Listen, Jenna. I only have a minute and I really need to speak to Gram."

Her sister finally got the hint and let the subject go. Moments later, Gram came to the phone. "Tori, honey, where are you?"

"I'm at a ranch near Brighton Valley. I told you, remember?"

"Oh…yes, I suppose you did. When are you coming home?"

"I'll be here for a while," Tori said. "But how are *you* doing, Gram?"

"Okay. The arthritis in my neck has been really bothering me, so Jenna's been doing most of the cooking and the housework. She's been so good to me."

"I'm glad to hear it."

"She also took me to see Sean," Gram added. "He's living with some other young men, and he's doing very well. He's so handsome. He looks a lot like your father did at his age."

Maybe so, but other than a physical resemblance, the

two couldn't be any more different. Still, it's not as though Tori wanted Sean to be doing badly. It's just that Gram believed anything he and Jenna told her:

"My homework is done."

"Yes, there'll be chaperones at the party."

"The school attendance clerk is lying. I was in school yesterday. You can ask my friends."

"Sean and Jenna are snowballing you," Tori used to tell her grandparents. But the older couple had never listened, saying only that Tori should cut her little brother and sister some slack.

Tori had known the younger kids needed a firm hand, so when she'd let them each move in with her, she'd thought she would be a positive influence on their lives.

Instead they'd been negative influences on hers.

But that was muddy water under a rickety bridge.

So she chatted with her grandmother for a while, trying to keep the focus on Gram, her health and her friends.

In the box in the corner, a couple of the kittens began to mew, letting Tori know it was time for their bedtime feeding.

"Listen," she told Gram. "I need to hang up now. But I'll give you a call in a couple of days."

After saying goodbye and disconnecting the line, Tori went to the kitchen to prepare the bottles of formula, where she found Granny seated at the round oak table, drinking a glass of milk and eating one of the gingersnap cookies Connie had made earlier.

"Good evening," Granny said. "Would you like to join me for a bedtime snack?"

"I'm afraid the babies are hungry, so I'd better see about them first."

"Is something wrong?" Granny asked. "When you first came in here, you were frowning."

Tori supposed her family burdens had caused some momentary stress, but she wasn't up to discussing them. Especially right before bed. It wouldn't make for a restful sleep. So she mustered a smile. "Everything's fine."

"How did your little talk with Matthew go this evening?" Granny took a sip of milk, her gaze rooted on Tori. "Was he in a better mood?"

"We had a nice chat. I think it was good for him to get out of the house." Tori pulled the little bottles from the cupboard and the kitten formula from the fridge. "Tomorrow morning I'm going to try and find a physical therapist in the area. He gave me reason to believe that he'd be open to making an appointment."

"Good." Granny fingered the white eyelet trim that adorned the bodice of her nightgown. "I'm glad to hear that. He might not be able to ride in the rodeo again, but at least he should be able to walk. His depression has had us all concerned."

"He must have really loved his fiancée," Tori said.

"I'm sure he was fond of her." Granny pushed back her chair, then got to her feet and shuffled to the cookie jar, where she pulled out a couple of gingersnaps, handing one to Tori. "But…well, she just wasn't quite…his type."

Tori took a bite of the cookie as she tried to decipher just what Granny meant by that.

"Have you ever been in love?" the older woman asked.

The question took Tori by surprise. She'd told Granny about James. And while they'd never discussed marriage, they had cared for each other.

Well, at least, that's what Tori had thought until James and her sister had betrayed her.

As she tried to come up with a truthful answer to Granny's question, all she could say was, "I'm not sure."

She'd had feelings for James. After all, their relationship wouldn't have taken a sexual turn if she hadn't.

But had she loved him?

"If what you'd felt was truly love," Granny said, "you wouldn't have had to think twice. There's a powerful zing in the heart that's impossible to deny."

Then, if that was the case, Tori's relationship with James had been lacking.

"I don't think Matt truly loved Cindy, either," Granny added. "But don't get me wrong. Cindy was a nice gal, and I'm sure Matt really liked her. It's just that I never thought they were suited for each other."

Matt must have thought so, Tori decided.

Why else would he have asked Cindy to marry him?

"Well," Granny said. "I'd better get some sleep. Morning will be here before we know it."

"Did you take your pills?" Tori asked.

Granny patted Tori on the arm. "Yes, I did. Thanks for the reminder. I haven't been forgetting to take them anymore. That little, plastic, seven-day container you gave me to use really helps."

As the older woman left the room, Tori cleaned up what little mess she'd made, then carried the bottles back to her bedroom.

She couldn't help thinking about what Granny had said regarding Matt's feelings for Cindy.

And she couldn't help disagreeing.

The man was a competitor by nature. After all, look at his chosen career. To ride wild, bucking broncos, he'd have to be a fighter.

He was also a survivor. She was reminded of the story he'd told her about living with his abusive uncle. She also thought about how feisty he'd been when he'd arrived at the Rocking C as a boy, but how he'd eventually made a place for himself.

Didn't it make more sense that, after a debilitating injury, he'd fight to get back what he'd lost? That he'd be determined to walk—if not ride—again?

No, the depression had to have been caused by grief over Cindy's death.

Granny had said they weren't suited. But what about the old adage that insisted opposites attract?

There was a lot that mothers and others who were sitting on the sidelines had no way of knowing.

Matt must have loved Cindy…a lot.

And Tori couldn't help being just a wee bit envious.

When she'd told James their relationship was over, he'd apologized about kissing Jenna, but he hadn't tried to talk Tori into giving him another chance. Not that she would have given him one. He'd shown his true colors.

But if Tori ever got involved with another man again, it would be with someone who loved her.

Someone who would at least grieve when she was gone.

The next day Tori located a physical therapist in Wexler, a town twenty miles north of Brighton Valley. She informed Matt and was relieved when he agreed to let her make an appointment for him.

So, on Thursday morning, the first available opening the therapist had, Tori woke up bright and early and gave the kittens their first feeding. As she did so, she took care to look over Tippy.

He seemed to be growing stronger, although he was still significantly smaller than the others. She was glad Matt had suggested they use an eyedropper to give him those initial feedings. It had made all the difference in the world.

In a sense, she thought of her and Matt as a team—at least when it came to the kittens. She just hoped that teamwork carried over to his therapy. It was important that she do whatever she could to get him back on his feet again. She owed that much to Granny.

She just hoped she hadn't met her match in the stubborn cowboy, especially when she feared he might never get over the loss of the woman he'd loved.

At nine o'clock she took Matt outside and tried to help him climb into the passenger side of the old ranch pickup.

"I can do it," he said.

She supposed, if he'd been taking showers, that he was managing on his own, but she wasn't sure if he was ready to put weight on his legs. Either way, she couldn't very well force him to accept her assistance.

Not when there was an issue of male pride.

As Matt struggled to get out of the chair and into the truck, his steps were unsteady, and his expression contorted in pain.

It was impossible to squelch the nurse in her. "Are you—"

"I'm *fine.*" He reached for the door, as well as the hood of the pickup. "I'm not an invalid."

She waited for him to get his entire body inside and close the door. Then she collapsed the wheelchair and placed it in back.

Moments later she climbed behind the wheel of the ten-year-old dual-wheeled Ford and began the forty-minute drive to Wexler.

A grimace continued to stretch across Matt's face, and she wasn't sure if it was because of pain or her interference. Maybe it was merely frustration because of how slow his recovery had been. Either way, she decided to bite her tongue until his mood improved.

So she focused on the smile that Granny wore this morning when she realized Matt was really going to finally start the physical therapy. It must be a big relief to know her youngest son was finally on a wellness track.

Just as Tori pulled onto the paved road that ran along the west side of the ranch, Matt reached for the radio knob, turned on the power and chose an FM station.

Tori had never been a huge fan of country-western music, but she couldn't help following the upbeat rhythm of the song that filled the inside of the cab. She was drawn to the words, to the romantic ballad about a love that was lost and rediscovered just before it was too late.

When the tune was over, the deejay, who referred to himself as "Shotgun" Bob Bridger, announced that he'd been playing the latest hit by Greg Clayton, a local boy who'd become one of the most promising performers in the business.

So that was the Clayton brother Tori had seen pictures of but hadn't met. The handsome, dark-haired entertainer whose musical talent was making him famous.

As she listened to the words and the melody, she could certainly understand why his fame was growing. There was something both soothing and alluring about Greg's voice, and it would have drawn her interest and attention even if he hadn't been one of Granny's boys.

"I really liked that song," she admitted. "Greg's musical ability shines. You must be proud of him."

"Yep. He's always had talent and been a showman. His success hasn't surprised anyone who knew him as a kid."

They made small talk as they traveled, but Matt continued to gaze out the window, his attention obviously elsewhere.

Tori wondered what he was thinking about but hated to pry. So she focused on the road as she followed the directions she'd gotten from MapQuest. She had a pretty good idea of where she was going, but when she pulled into the driveway of the medical building she'd been looking for, a white BMW came flying out of nowhere, and she had to slam on her brakes to avoid a collision.

The screeching halt caused them both to lurch forward against the shoulder straps of their seat belts. The blonde driving the Beemer merely mouthed an "Oops" and gave a toodle-dee-doo wave of her fingers before proceeding onto the street.

"Damn," Matt said. "Didn't you see her?"

"No, I didn't."

He mumbled something about women drivers, and she hoped he was commenting about the blond chick driving the BMW.

If he'd been lumping both of them together, she wanted to defend herself. She'd avoided a crash, hadn't she?

She opened her mouth to launch a retort, then thought better of it and clamped her lips shut. Matt didn't need to think about car accidents, especially when he was still recovering from the fatal collision he'd had.

"Do you see an empty parking space?" she asked.

"Nope. Not in front."

There was, however, a spot with a handicap sign. She wouldn't actually shut off the engine, since she didn't have the official decals or plates, but she couldn't imagine anyone complaining once they saw Matt get into the wheelchair.

"I'll let you out right here," she said. "Then I'll meet you inside. That is, unless you need some help with the door."

"I can get it."

While the truck idled, she slid out of the driver's seat and removed the chair from the back. In the meantime, Matt swung his legs around and proceeded to get out of the pickup.

Tori waited for him to settle into the seat, then asked, "Do you want me to push you into the lobby?"

"No." He shot her a frown. "In case you haven't figured it out, I don't like being pushed."

Something told her he was talking about more than having her assistance while he was in the chair. And she supposed she had been pushing him a bit as it was.

She blew out a little sigh, telling herself that she'd at least gotten him to Wexler and to his first physical therapy appointment.

And she'd done so *safely,* even if he didn't quite agree.

"After I park, I'll meet you inside," she said again, ready to circle back to the driver's seat.

"Nope. I'm going in alone." He nodded to a grassy area

near the front of the building, where a bench sat in the shade of a tree. "You can wait over there or in the pickup. Or run some errands and come back for me."

"Okay, but I thought it might help if I… Well, if I went inside and talked to them, they could show me what exercises you need to work on, and we could do them at home."

"I'm a big boy, Tori." The gentle blue of his eyes mocked the gruffness in his tone. "I don't need a personal nurse, whether you think I do or not."

He was right, of course. So why did she feel compelled to continue offering her services?

She told herself it was out of consideration for his mother. But she feared it might be more than that.

As Matt wheeled himself toward the smoked-glass lobby door, she stood beside the idling pickup and watched the ex-rodeo cowboy go.

A part of her sympathized, yet another part actually admired him.

The sun glistened off the glossy gold strands of his hair, as the well-developed muscles in his upper shoulders and arms worked to propel him to the entrance. He stopped long enough to push the square metallic button that swung open the automatic doors.

As she continued to watch him go, a shiver of heat ran through her blood and an unwelcome jolt of attraction struck low in her belly. She tried her best to shake it off.

It was too soon for her to have those kinds of feelings and thoughts again. Wasn't it? Only six months had passed since she'd suffered that ugly breakup, thanks to her younger sister.

Okay, so it had been James's fault, too.

And maybe she would have come to the conclusion that their relationship hadn't been made in heaven, that it hadn't been destined to last.

That wasn't the point.

Still, she needed time to heal and recover without complications. So, finding herself attracted to Matt Clayton was just an indication that she was on the rebound. Why, any man would look good to her now.

Of course, she had to admit that no one else had looked the least bit interesting to her before this wounded cowboy.

Chapter Six

Matt hadn't meant to be rude by shutting Tori out when she obviously had only wanted to be helpful. But before going into physical therapy, he hadn't been sure what he was up against.

He also wanted to hear what the therapist had to say and to be able to ponder without an audience any orders the doctor had given.

So he'd chosen to go inside alone, and now he had the option to decide what—if anything—he wanted to share with Tori.

As it was, he was glad she hadn't been with him.

After assessing Matt's balance, strength and range of motion, the therapist had worked him over thoroughly, and the process had been torturous. But Matt pushed himself hard, and as a result his hips, legs and ankles hurt like hell. In fact, he felt as though he'd been trampled under the hooves of an unbroken stallion.

"It might be best to take some pain medication before your next appointment," Stan Granger, the therapist, had said.

Matt said he would, yet a part of him felt as though he deserved the ache and discomfort, as though that might somehow be fitting and just.

"You can start putting some weight on your legs now," Stan said, "but only for short periods of time each day. And when you do, you'll need to use a walker."

The idea, Stan explained, was to gradually build up Matt's strength and balance.

Now, as Matt wheeled himself out of the lobby and into the natural light of day, he scanned the grassy area, looking for Tori.

He spotted her seated sideways on a bench, reading a book. She looked pretty sitting there, her legs stretched out along the seat, one knee bent. She'd tucked her hair behind an ear, giving him a glimpse of her profile, and he couldn't help slowing himself to a stop so he could watch her for a moment or two.

Her brow was furrowed, and she nibbled on her bottom lip. The words on the pages obviously held some kind of fascination for her, and he suddenly wished he was standing behind her, reading over her shoulder to see what had caught her interest.

Instead he began the slow process of wheeling toward her. If she offered to push him this time, he just might let her.

Of course he'd never ask.

He maneuvered the chair toward the place where the sidewalk met the grass, just steps away from the bench on which she sat.

At the sound of his approach, she glanced up and smiled. She lifted her hand to shade the sun from her eyes. "How did it go?"

"All right."

She studied him as though trying to determine whether he was being truthful, but he figured his sweat-dampened hair and the perspiration on his shirt ought to be pretty convincing.

"It looks to me like someone gave you quite a workout," she said.

"You've got that right." He blew out a raspy sigh. "But if it helps me get out of this damn chair, then it was well worth the effort."

"I'm glad to hear you say that."

He nodded toward the open paperback novel that rested in her lap. "What are you reading?"

Her cheeks had taken on a rosy hue, either from the sun or embarrassment; he couldn't be sure.

She smiled shyly. "I found a book lying on the grass. Someone must have left it. And I…"

Matt looked at the front cover that sported a bare-chested male, his biceps bulging. The top button of his jeans was undone.

A grin tugged at Matt's lips. He suspected that the flush on Tori's cheeks wasn't from the sun after all, but rather from the sexy novel she'd been caught reading.

"Did they give you exercises to do at home?" she asked, getting to her feet.

She placed the book in her purse.

Not back on the grass where she'd found it?

A grin stole across his face. Obviously, she was enjoying the sexy story and meant to finish it at home.

"Yep."

"Lord knows I'd never want to push a man who hates to be pushed," she said with a smile, drawing him away from his erotic musings. "But the offer still stands. If you'd like me to work with you, all you have to do is ask."

Actually, now that he'd met with Stan and realized how tough physical therapy was going to be, how hard he'd have to work at home…

But Matt was never one to admit needing help.

"When is your next appointment?" she asked.

"A week from today."

They started toward the pickup, and her steps slowed as though she wanted to offer to get behind his chair and help again, but she must have thought better of it.

It would have been nice to kick back and rest his aching muscles, though. And for a moment he was almost sorry that she'd reconsidered.

"Do you need to get back to the ranch right away?" he asked.

"No. Why?"

Matt would have preferred to go straight home, but it had seemed like forever since he'd had a decent meal. And even the abundance of sweets was getting old.

He wanted a big, juicy steak, a double helping of French fries and… Heck, he'd even settle for a helping of vegetables, which had never been something he particularly liked. But if they were cooked properly…

"Let's stop in Brighton Valley at Caroline's," he said. "If you don't mind taking our time getting home, I'll treat you to lunch."

"You've got a deal." She tossed him a pretty smile, then waited for him to slide into the passenger side.

It hadn't been easy getting into the vehicle the first time, when they'd been back at the ranch and just starting out. But after that workout, Matt's legs felt as though they were going to buckle at any moment.

And as luck would have it, they damn near did.

Tori, who'd pushed the chair out of the way, stood between him and the door. Apparently sensing a catastrophe ready to happen, she grabbed him just in the nick of time, providing some extra support.

She was stronger than he'd given her credit for.

Softer and warmer, too.

The scent of her shampoo and body lotion, something tropical, snaked around him like a serpent in paradise. And if he didn't have that god-awful pain shooting through his legs, he might have actually enjoyed the awkward yet sensual embrace.

"Are you okay?" she asked.

"Yeah," he said through gritted teeth. "Thanks."

He hated to admit it—Matt Clayton didn't *need* anyone—but if it hadn't been for her quick response, he would have fallen down. And then he might have been in one hell of a fix.

Of course, he was in a different kind of "fix" right now.

Her breasts pressed tauntingly against his side, and as her arms tightened around his waist, a jolt of heat rushed through his blood.

Great.

This was neither the time nor the place for sexual awareness, especially since he wasn't comfortable with his current vulnerability, so he tried to laugh it off.

"I'd like it a whole lot better if I weren't temporarily incapacitated," he said. "I might have copped a feel."

Those cheeks flushed again, a deep telltale shade of pink. And he couldn't tell whether she was flattered or uncomfortable because of his remark.

Flattered, he hoped. Because for the first time in what seemed like forever, he was thinking about something and someone other than Cindy and how he'd failed her.

And interestingly enough, the thought of a sexual romp with Tori promised to work a hell of a lot better than the pain meds or Jack Daniels ever had.

Ten minutes later Tori pulled the pickup in front of Caroline's Diner and parked in the shade of one of the elm trees that lined the street.

Other than the music playing on the radio, the fifteen-minute drive to Brighton Valley had been quiet and uneventful. She suspected it was because things had gotten a little…awkward after Matt had almost fallen while getting into the truck.

Thank goodness she'd been standing beside him when it happened.

As a nurse, she'd always had to be on her toes, so instinct had kicked in.

Of course, it was a different kind of instinct taking the lead when she had her arms wrapped around him.

Being so close, only a breath and a heartbeat away,

she'd caught the hint of fresh perspiration that mingled with the woodsy scent of his cologne. Something primal and distinctly feminine had sparked inside her, and when he'd joked about copping a feel, she'd actually found the idea intriguing. Exciting.

So what was with that?

It was enough to force her to keep her eyes on the road ahead as she drove to the diner, yet she couldn't help stealing glances across the seat at Matt, who repeatedly stroked his thighs.

She suspected he was still feeling the stretch and burn from therapy and wanted to comment about it. But she kept her mouth shut.

If she'd learned anything about him it was that he resented her help and interference. So she'd have to be content to know that he was at least making strides in the right direction, that he was finally doing his part to recover.

"We're lucky the lunch crowd already came and went," Matt said, as he scanned the front of the diner and seemed to note a few empty parking spaces. "There's usually a wait."

"That must mean that the food is every bit as good as you said it was. What kind of things are on the menu?"

"Baked chicken, pork chops, country-fried steak. You name it. And Caroline's mashed potatoes are just the way Granny used to make them. The desserts are good, too."

"Sounds wonderful."

"It is. And you can't beat the price. If you want a real treat and a bargain to boot, read the chalkboard that's set up by the cash register."

"Is that where she advertises the special of the day?"

"Yep. But it always says, 'What the sheriff ate.'"

"I don't get it," Tori said.

Matt chuckled. "The sheriff is Caroline's husband."

Tori got out of the truck. When she had the wheelchair set up, she pushed it to the passenger side.

"I'm willing to help you out if you want me to," she said, trying to make light of the fact that he'd pushed his legs to the limit already today. "But you'll have to promise not to cop a feel."

"No way." Matt lobbed her a grin that matched the one she was wearing. "I don't make promises I don't plan to keep."

A flood of warmth spread across her cheeks, and the thought of him touching her, caressing her, shot a jolt of heat to her core.

He was joking, of course.

Wasn't he?

She opened the door for him and waited as he maneuvered the chair inside. It was fortunate that Caroline's Diner provided handicap access. Tori hadn't been there since the day she'd met Granny, and it was almost like seeing it for the first time. Maybe because she was seeing it through Matt's eyes.

She scanned the small restaurant with its pale-yellow walls and white eyelet café window coverings. Tables dotted the center of the room, and brown vinyl booths lined the perimeter. An old-fashioned counter with swivel seats faced the kitchen.

The chalkboard Matt had told her about stood near the register and was hard to miss. Sure enough, in a feminine script, it was noted what the sheriff had eaten: meat loaf;

country-mashed potatoes; buttered, garden-fresh green beans; and peach cobbler. The price listed was $6.99.

"I'm going to start with the special," Matt said. "Then I'm going to order something else."

Tori arched a brow in question.

"Hey, I'm dying for a decent meal. And God only knows when I'll get another chance to fill up again."

A blond matronly woman at the back of the diner was handing a bill to an elderly man seated at one of the booths, his back to the entrance. As the waitress glanced up at Matt and Tori, she swept her arm in Vanna-White-style. "Feel free to sit anywhere, folks."

"How's this?" Tori pointed to the first table they came to.

"Perfect."

She removed a chair so Matt could wheel in close.

"Well, as I live and breathe," a salt-and-pepper-haired woman said from the kitchen. "Matthew Clayton. You're a sight for sore eyes."

"Hey, Caroline." Matt flashed the woman a grin. "I hope those local boys didn't eat all that peach cobbler."

"I've got just enough left for a couple of helpings." The proprietor's friendly smile faded to sympathy and concern. "How ya doin', hon?"

Matt's grin faltered a bit. "Don't worry about me. I'll be back to fighting weight before you know it."

"That's good," Caroline said. "What can I get you?"

"Do you want the special, too?" he asked Tori.

Actually, she hadn't eaten a good meat loaf in ages. "Sure."

"We'll start by having what the sheriff ate," he told Caroline.

About that time, the silver-haired gentleman who'd been seated at the booth in the rear slowly got to his feet and made his way to their table.

It was Dr. Graham.

He walked a bit stooped, but his eyes and smile were bright as he extended a liver-spotted hand to Matt. "It's good to see you out and about, son."

"Hey, Doc." Matt greeted the man, then introduced him to Tori.

"We've already met," Dr. Graham said, turning his attention to Tori. "How's Joey doing?"

"Sabrina said he's improving every day."

"Glad to hear it." Dr. Graham crossed his arms and gave Tori a once-over. "You know, I was talking to Edna the other day and told her that she ought to encourage you to go back to school and get a medical degree. You'd make one heck of a doctor."

"Thanks. That's quite a compliment and it's certainly an idea to consider." But even if Tori had already put enough distance between her and the past, it was out of the question. She didn't have the time or the money to pursue medical school.

"I'm not going to be around forever," Dr. Graham said. "And when I finally take down my shingle, I'd like to know that folks around here have another physician to keep them healthy."

Matt seemed to sit back and take it all in. "But then we'd lose our personal nurse at the Rocking C."

"Well, now, that's a point I hadn't thought about. You need your own private nurse, Matthew Clayton." Dr.

Graham chuckled. "And I said as much to your mother years ago."

"Why is that?" Tori asked, glad to steer the subject to something she'd rather discuss.

"Edna had to drag Matt into my office for one injury or another. He was always risking his neck doing some fool thing—often on a dare or a bet. As a boy, he was determined to make a place for himself on the ranch and made a habit of trying to prove himself as the fastest and the strongest of the Clayton boys." A slow grin stretched across the old doctor's craggy face, and his gray eyes glimmered. "How many stitches did you end up getting after that that crazy piebald mare threw you into the fence?"

"Only twelve."

Doc grinned. "You know, I told you while I cleaned your scalp that you'd better stay away from unbroken horses. And I swear, that must have been the wrong thing to say to a boy who never backed down from a challenge. Your mother said from that day forward you dug in your heels and swore up and down you'd be a rodeo cowboy. I never did know a young person to be so cantankerous and dead set on proving himself."

"So let me get this right." Tori placed her arms on the table and leaned toward Matt. "You chose a career based on someone telling you that you couldn't or shouldn't do it?"

Before Matt could respond, Doc said, "I wouldn't go that far. Matthew always was a natural-born horseman, and when he became a champion bronc rider, it was no surprise to anyone. But he's got a stubborn streak, that's for sure."

"I've seen it." Tori's gaze snagged Matt's, and something warm and fluid pooled between them, something she feared she might drown in if she wasn't careful.

Fortunately, Doc offered her what amounted to a flotation device. "Did Matt ever tell you why he always jumped at the chance to drive into town to pick up the ranch supplies?"

"No," Tori said. "Why?"

"Apparently, late at night while everyone slept, he rebuilt the engine on one of the old ranch pickups. It wasn't long before he became a teenage legend in these parts by giving every hotrod in town a run for its money. And if he couldn't find any competitors to eat his dust along the county road, he'd play chicken with the freight train that passed through each day."

"That sounds pretty reckless," she said.

"Maybe so," Matt admitted. "But I always had a handle on my limitations."

As his words hovered in the air, she could see him withdraw and grow solemn. Distant.

She assumed he was thinking about his injuries, about his inability to ever ride bucking broncos again. If she were his wife or lover, she'd be a little bit glad about that.

Yet she'd be sad, too.

Banning a man like Matt from the rodeo, from the thing he loved most in the world, would be like hobbling a wild stallion.

And in that sense, she supposed he had a lot in common with her.

So she opted to change the subject—for both of them.

"By the way, Dr. Graham, Matt and I are having a surprise birthday party for Granny in a couple of weeks.

You'll be getting an invitation soon, but I hope you'll help us keep it a secret. She's pretty sharp."

Doc laughed. "You can say that again. I've known Edna for nigh on sixty years, give or take a few. And that woman catches more in the air than most folks do with both feet on the ground. Sometimes I swear she's got an extra set of eyes in the back of her head."

Moments later, Caroline personally brought out their meals, and Doc excused himself, saying he had to get back to his office. He had a full schedule of patients this afternoon.

Two of the first things Tori had noted about the elderly doctor had been his dedication and his stamina. And each time she was around him and watched him work, she was impressed with the skill he'd amassed over the past half century by treating those in the community. And she couldn't help admiring him.

The people in and around Brighton Valley were sure going to miss him when he retired.

As she took the first bite of her lunch, she closed her eyes and savored the mouthwatering flavor of homemade meat loaf. Her mother used to cook meals like this—down home and from scratch—but it had been a long time since Tori had tasted the like. Her grandmother had never been as gifted. Of maybe she had, but she'd just grown tired of slaving away in the kitchen when the younger kids insisted upon fast food and pizza.

"You were right," Tori told Matt. "This food is divine."

When they'd both finished eating, Matt paid the bill. Then they went through the extra motions and effort it took to get Matt out of the chair and into the pickup.

Before Tori could start the engine, she noticed an office supply store that was just two doors down from the diner.

"Do you mind if I run inside and pick up some printed paper and matching envelopes to use for the invitations?"

"No. Go ahead."

Ten minutes later, they were on the open road and driving toward the ranch.

Another Greg Clayton song came over the airwaves, and Tori found herself falling easily into the beat. No wonder he was gaining fans right and left. Soon she would have to count herself as one of them.

"Do you think Greg will be able to make it to the party?" she asked. "I imagine he's pretty busy."

"I'll give him a call. He loves Granny as much as Jared and I do, so I'm sure he'll do his best to at least make a showing."

"Good."

When they arrived at the ranch, Tori parked the pickup where she'd found it, then shut off the ignition.

She was torn between offering to help Matt get out and respecting his pride. Either way, she had to get the wheel-chair for him.

Thank goodness he'd be able to use a walker soon.

After unfolding the chair and pushing it to the passenger door, she waited as Matt slid out of the seat and got to his feet.

He grimaced, and she decided to heck with his pride. There was no way she wanted to risk having him fall after such a full and undoubtedly tiring day.

So she reached for him, then hesitated.

He turned slightly, his gaze zeroing in on hers providing her a glimpse of the man inside. The man who refused to be beaten by anyone or anything.

A man who could take a woman's breath away with a smile.

She expected him to settle into the chair, but instead, he released his grip on the top of the vehicle door and ran the knuckles of one hand along her cheek in a sensual caress.

A whisper of goose bumps ran up and down her arms, and her lips parted.

As she sucked in a breath she'd forgotten to take, his hand slowly dropped, skimming along her neck, down her chest and nearly grazing one of her breasts.

Still, her nipple contracted, her pulse spiked, and her breath caught again.

A rebellious grin tugged at his lips and his gaze slid into the very heart of her.

Then he lowered his butt into the chair and began to maneuver himself to the back of the house, where the ramp would allow him entrance.

But Tori remained rooted to the spot, caught up in his sensual gaze and in the flutter of pheromones he'd set off overhead.

She'd thought he'd been kidding about copping a feel. And she supposed he had been playing around. Taunting her.

Yet she couldn't help wondering if he'd actually touch her one day…

And hoping that he would.

Chapter Seven

The next day, a hospital supply company stopped by the ranch and dropped off a rental walker for Matt to use.

Stan had suggested that Matt slowly build up his strength, venturing from the wheelchair for a few minutes each day, but Matt decided to push harder than that and used the aluminum-framed walker as often as his bones and muscles could stand.

He knew he was doing more than the therapist had wanted him to, but he couldn't help it. When he set his mind on something, he went after it—just as he had when he'd overstepped his bounds with Tori and pretended to cop a feel.

Under the circumstances, with their relationship being what it was—platonic—it had been inappropriate.

It had started out as a joke, but as his knuckles stroked

the silk of her skin and her breath caught in a sensual response, her gaze had locked on his and turned the entire world inside out.

At that very moment, touching her had seemed like the most natural thing in the world to do.

Not that he needed to get involved in another relationship again. He'd gradually come to the conclusion that the last one had been a mistake from the get-go—and for a multitude of reasons. But that wasn't something he'd ever admit.

Because, if he did, it would make the unnecessary deaths of Cindy and her son even tougher for him to bear, and the guilt he carried even more crippling.

So Matt and Tori had just gone about their lives as though nothing had happened, as though nothing had changed.

"Do you want to take a walk?" she'd asked him during dinner.

He couldn't see why not. There was no reason to remain cooped up inside the house any longer. "Sure."

"You probably should use the wheelchair," she'd added. "That might be easier for you."

Now that he'd started therapy, he wasn't so sure he wanted to opt for easy. Not if it slowed down the recovery period. But he wasn't sure how far he could go outdoors, especially in the dark.

"Whatever," he'd said, unwilling to admit his weakness.

So after dinner, Tori took the wicker rocker, the table and the citronella candle from the front porch and set them up near the barn, obviously thinking that she and Matt would chat as they had last time.

And that was okay with him. To be honest, he'd

begun to enjoy her company. So after he maneuvered the chair down the ramp at the back door, they started their walk.

The moon wasn't as bright as it had been the other night, but the sights and smells of the ranch had the same, invigorating effect on Matt.

"I'd like to send out the party invitations tomorrow," Tori said. "Did you get a guest list made?"

"Yes. And I talked to Greg. He's on tour this month, but he'll be able to fly in for the day. He'll have to leave that night, though. I also called Jared, who asked if there was anything he could do. So I told him to come early and be prepared to work. There'll be a lot to set up in the barn—assuming you're still dead set on having it there."

She'd changed her mind a half-dozen times, unable to decide on the best setting. But she'd finally settled on the area just outside the back of the barn because it was closer to the house and the bathroom.

"The barn will also give us a place to hide everything. After Granny leaves the ranch for church, we can open up the back doors and set out the tables under that big sycamore."

"All right." Matt glanced up at the moon, saw that it was starting to wane. "By the way, I also made a couple of calls, and Red Filkins, a rancher who lives about five miles south of here, has a buckboard he'll let us use. Since you want to make this party a complete surprise, we'll need to ask people to park away from the house. So I figure it'll still come in handy as a shuttle."

"Good."

As they continued their walk, he wished that he was

strolling along beside her, that he could brush his shoulder against hers and risk touching her again.

But that was a fool idea.

He supposed it was best that his grip was on the wheels of the chair. God knew he didn't need to get any more touchy-feely with one of his mother's employees, no matter how pretty she was.

"What about food?" Tori asked. "With a western theme, it would be nice to have barbecue or something Tex-Mex."

"Either way, we'll need to get a caterer," Matt said. "There's no way we can have Connie fix the food."

Tori furrowed her brow and bit down on her bottom lip.

She was probably worried about hurting the cook's feelings, but there was no way Matt would invite his mother's friends to a party and feed them crappy food.

"Connie is a really nice person," Tori said. "And she's got enough to worry about with a baby on the way and no husband or any family support."

Matt slowed the pace and stopped. "I would be tactful when telling her. We'll just say that we don't want to burden her with all that work, especially since she's expecting. Maybe we can ask her to whip up a couple of cakes instead."

Tori brightened. "That's a wonderful idea. Then she'd feel as though she was contributing something."

"Why don't you talk to her, then. And suggest that she bake about ten or twelve of those Texas chocolate cakes she made last week."

"Ten or twelve?" Tori turned to face him. "How many people are you planning to invite?"

"I don't know. Fifty, I guess. But I want to make sure there's plenty to eat."

"With that many people, we'll have to rent tables and chairs. And since we'll need a caterer, do you have any idea who we should contact?"

"I'm going to call Chuck's Wagon."

"Who?"

"It's a guy who has this traveling barbecue setup," Matt explained. "He'll provide chicken and beef, coleslaw, beans, potato salad, corn on the cob. It'll be perfect. You'll see."

"All right. But you might want to contact him tomorrow. He might be busy already."

"Will do." Matt started down the road again, but his wheels hit a soft spot of dirt. "Dammit."

"Do you need help?" she asked.

"No, I'll…" It was more of a struggle than he'd antici-pated, but he'd be darned if he was going to ask for help.

Nevertheless, she got behind him and pushed.

"Why don't we turn around," he said. "There are probably more soft spots up ahead."

This time she let him maneuver the chair by himself.

He hated being wheelchair-bound, hated being depen-dent. Of course, what he hated most of all was the thought that he'd never be able to ride in the rodeo again.

He shot a glance at Tori, wondering if she understood why it was so important for him to do things on his own.

Maybe.

"Do you miss it?" he asked.

She turned to him, brows furrowed. "Miss what?"

"Nursing."

Her lips parted. "I…well, I…Yes, I do. Why do you ask?"

"No real reason, I suppose." They continued to move

toward the table and chair she'd set up when they first began their walk. "It seems pretty clear to everyone who's met you that you were cut out for the medical field."

Just as Matt had been born to ride broncs, he supposed.

She seemed to think on his assumption for a while, then said, "Like I told you before, I needed a break. That's all. I'll go back someday."

"Something tells me that it wasn't a matter of burnout or boredom that sent you to Brighton Valley."

She didn't respond, but that didn't stop him from speculating.

Maybe she felt responsible for someone's death. Maybe she lay awake each night and wondered what she could have done differently.

And kicked herself because she hadn't.

If that were the case, she and Matt had a lot more in common than he'd realized.

Two weeks later, the day of the surprise party dawned sunny and bright. As far as Matt could tell, Granny didn't have a clue that a celebration had been planned in her honor.

For one reason, her actual birthday was still a week away.

Today he sat on the front porch, the walker parked near the wicker chair on which he rocked in a carefree manner. Once Granny was gone, he suspected the party preparations would kick into high gear. Tori had created a list of who was to do what and at what time. He'd never seen a woman so organized.

As he heard the drone of an engine coming down the drive, he glanced at his wristwatch—9:45 and right on time.

It was Sunday, and as had become the weekly routine

for almost as long as Matt could remember, Hilda Det-weiler, a friend of Granny's, came by the ranch in her red '86 Cadillac Seville.

Hilda used to own and operate the Pampered Lady Beauty Parlor in Brighton Valley, which she sold when she retired. But she still continued to work part-time out of her home, where she cut and styled the hair of some of her oldest and best customers.

Granny was one of them.

Ever since Granny's husband, Everett, had died, Hilda made it a point to stop by and take Granny to church. Unless something came up that required one of them to go home early, the two friends usually made a day of it by eating lunch at Caroline's Diner and then driving into Wexler for a shopping trip or to see a movie.

Today, Hilda was going to feign a headache after lunch.

As the red Caddy pulled to a stop just steps away from the front porch, the perfectly coiffed silver-haired lady tapped her horn twice to announce her arrival to Granny. Then she rolled down the window of her car. "Hello, Matthew."

"Hey, Hilda. How's it going?"

"Not bad for an old woman. Edna told me you've been getting out of that wheelchair some. I was happy to hear it."

Before Matt could respond, the screen door swung open and Granny started down the steps, the handle of her white handbag draped over her forearm.

"You're welcome to come with us, Matt," his mother said on her way to Hilda's car. "We've got a visiting minister speaking, and he's supposed to be entertaining as well as informative."

"Thanks, but I'll pass. I never was able to sit through a complete sermon." Every time his mother would drag him and his brothers to church, he'd have a million reasons to get up.

Granny chuckled. "That's for sure."

"Have fun," Matt said. "What movie are you going to see?"

"Probably that new one with Ben Stiller. We both like him."

"Let me know what you ladies think of it," Matt said. "I just might catch a ride into town and see it myself."

Granny paused beside the open passenger door of Hilda's car. "You know, I never could figure why you could sit through a two-hour movie but couldn't handle a thirty-minute sermon."

Matt winked at Hilda. "The trick is to stuff me full of popcorn."

Both women shook their heads and chuckled as Granny climbed into the passenger seat. Moments later, the red Cadillac was kicking up dust and gravel along the drive while the silver-haired duo headed for Brighton Valley.

"Is it safe now?" Tori asked, as she poked her head out the screen door and stepped onto the porch.

"Yep. They're gone."

In a matter of minutes, Tori had everyone on the ranch rounded up and assigned their respective jobs.

Connie brought out the bags of party supplies the women had hidden in one of the closets, and soon the ranch was buzzing with activity as they all readied for the arrival of the guests.

Everyone except Matt.

He wasn't able to do much and, as a result, felt about as worthless as a three-dollar bill. So, for that reason, he remained on the porch and watched the others turn the barn into a reception area for Granny's neighbors and friends.

Less than twenty minutes later, a white truck from the party-rental place brought the tables and chairs Matt had ordered. The heavy-set, straw-haired guy who'd been driving said, "I'm looking for Mr. Clayton."

"You found him."

"Good. I'm going to need a signature." The driver carried a clipboard up the steps and handed the paperwork to Matt, who scanned the figures to make sure they'd brought what he'd ordered and at the quoted price.

Satisfied that everything was right, Matt signed his name.

Before long, the tables and chairs were set up behind the barn, and the truck was on its way back to town.

Connie, who'd been outside helping Tori with the decorations, crossed the yard and climbed the steps onto the porch. "I'm going inside. Can I bring you something, Matt? Iced tea, maybe?"

He supposed it was nice of her to offer. And while he'd rather throw back something stronger than tea, something to numb the dark mood he'd begun to slip into as he watched the action going on around him, he wouldn't risk morphing into a jerk and ruining Granny's celebration. "Sure, Connie. Thanks. Tea sounds good. Would you mind putting some sugar in it?"

"Not at all." She went into the house, letting the screen shut behind her, just as the engine of an approaching car sounded.

Matt turned to see a black sedan coming down the

drive. He didn't recognize the vehicle, but when it pulled to a stop, he immediately spotted the driver and his mood suddenly lifted.

It was his brother behind the wheel. Joe Riley, Greg's buddy and the band's drummer, sat in the passenger seat.

Greg parked, then got out of the car wearing dark glasses, a black shirt, faded jeans and designer western boots. The moment he laid eyes on Matt, a million-dollar smile busted over his face.

He climbed the stairs and stuck out an arm. "Hey, little brother. How you doin'?"

Matt glanced down at the chair in which he was stuck. "I've been better. But let's talk about you. They're playing your latest release almost hourly on the radio. So my guess is that things are going pretty damn well."

"I can't complain."

"Are you sure you'll still need to leave tonight?"

"Yeah. I flew in from Louisville at eleven o'clock, rented the car and drove out here. I've arranged to meet the tour bus in Nashville in the morning. So I've got to head back to Houston tonight. I want to be close to the airport for an early flight out tomorrow."

"I'm glad you were able to work this out. Granny's going to be happy to see you." Matt leaned back in his seat, wishing he could stand and give his brother a welcoming hug. As it was, he'd feel funny doing so in this position. While he and his brothers were growing up they always seemed to be competing with each other about one thing or another and trying to prove who was top dog. And right now Matt felt as though he'd rolled over and taken the submissive, belly-up position.

Not that Greg or Jared lorded over him anymore. But as a kid it was important to him to be respected. To be looked up to.

Hell, he guessed it still was.

"I'm not going to be able to stay very long." Greg removed his sunglasses and lowered his gaze to meet Matt's. "Just long enough to wish Granny a happy birthday and sing a couple of songs."

"Great. Where's your guitar?"

"In the back seat of the car."

Joe, who was making his way from the parked sedan to the porch, laughed. "Greg doesn't go many places without that thing. I told him he ought to insure it with Lloyd's of London."

"Very funny." Greg glanced through the screen door. "Where's Jared?"

"He should be here any minute. By the way, our big brother, the one who swore never to get serious about a woman again, has fallen head over heart for Granny's bookkeeper."

"No kidding?" Greg tossed Matt a crooked grin. "That's great."

"Her name is Sabrina."

Before Matt could continue, the screen door swung open, and Connie stepped out carrying a glass of iced tea. She seemed to balk, then continued the motions she'd started.

"Greg," Matt said, "this is Connie, the new cook."

"Nice to meet you." Greg's gaze zeroed in on the petite, shapely woman, but she seemed to take it in stride.

She managed a casual nod and a slight smile. "How do you do."

Weird, Matt thought. Most women fell all over themselves when meeting Greg, especially if they sensed that he had any interest in them at all.

Connie had all but averted her eyes from him during the introductions. Then she excused herself and went back into the house.

"Is she married or something?" Greg asked, apparently getting the same vibe Matt had gotten.

Actually, Matt wasn't sure of her marital status, although he knew she was pregnant, which might explain her lack of interest.

If Matt thought his brother was actually interested in Connie, he would have shared that tidbit of information. But Greg had his choice of women, even if you didn't count the groupies.

"Maybe she hates country-western music," Joe said, crossing his arms and shifting his weight to one hip. "She probably doesn't even know who you are."

No, Matt thought. That couldn't be it. Granny didn't make any secret about how proud she was of her sons, pointing out that Jared ran an impressive spread up north, that Matt was a champion bronc rider and Greg's latest song had hit the top of the charts.

Of course, Connie always kept a low profile around the ranch. Maybe she was just shy.

"It doesn't matter," Greg said. "Besides, it's kind of nice to be able to check out an attractive woman and not have her throw herself at me."

"Speaking of attractive women—" Joe blew out a whistle "—this place is jumping with 'em."

Matt followed Joe's gaze to Tori, who was striding

toward them, wisps of her curly red hair falling from the bun in which she'd secured it. A flush on her cheeks told him she'd been rushing around trying to get everything just so.

As she approached, she wiped her hands against her hips. "We're trying to keep the vehicles parked along the dirt road that goes to the fishing pond so Granny won't immediately see them when she returns. Would you mind moving your car?"

"No problem." Joe flashed her a grin that suggested he'd do anything she asked.

"Tori," Matt said, "this is my brother Greg and his friend Joe."

She reached out a hand, and blessed Greg with the warmth Connie hadn't been able to muster. "It's nice to finally meet you, Greg. Your mom is so proud of you. Actually, she's proud of all her boys."

Matt wondered how his mother was going to be able to boast about him now that he was no longer able to compete. A slow ache settled in his chest.

Almost as if homing in on his discomfort, Tori turned to him. "Are you going to change your clothes, Matt?"

He glanced down at what he was wearing—faded jeans and a white cotton shirt—then back at her. "What's wrong with what I have on?"

"Nothing. I just thought that I would head inside, take a shower and get dressed. And if you wanted to do the same thing, I was going to offer my help."

"I'll stick with what I have on."

"All right." She tossed Joe and Greg a pretty smile. "It was nice meeting you both. I'll see you in a bit."

She headed into the house. As the door shut behind her, Joe uttered, "Damn, Matt. You're slipping."

Greg chuckled. "It sounded as though she was offering to undress you, invite you into her shower and scrub your back."

Matt chuffed. "She meant she'd reach the hangers in the closet or the drawers in the chest."

"I don't know about *that...*" Joe laughed.

"You guys are crazy." Still, Matt thought about the image of Tori removing his clothes, taking him by the hand and leading him into a hot, steamy shower. Of water sluicing down their naked bodies, soap sliding along each and every curve...

Damn. If he wasn't careful, he was going to need a shower all right—a cold one.

"No wonder you came back to stay at the Rocking C rather than with Jared," Greg said.

Actually, Jared had taken Sabrina and Joey back to his ranch and left Matt with Granny. There hadn't been any options. Jared had told Matt to take over Granny's books until Sabrina was able to return.

"Well," Joe said, "we'd better move that car before she comes back. You know what they say about redheads and their fiery tempers."

Ten minutes later the sedan had been moved, and Greg had made his way to the barn, his trademark guitar strapped over his shoulder.

Matt wondered if he ought to go back into the house so he could wheel himself down the ramp in back and head into the yard. People would be arriving soon, and he didn't want to be seated on the porch like an invalid.

As he maneuvered the chair around, he could hear Greg strumming his guitar, and a Texas two-step harmony floated through the air from the barn to the house. It was the kind of song that had a foot-tapping beat and compelled a man to grab a special lady by the hand and head out to the dance floor.

Just as Matt reached for the doorknob, Tori beat him to it, swinging open the screen. She was wearing a light-yellow sundress that reminded him of a field of daffodils. She wore a pretty shade of lipstick, and her curly hair had been pulled into a neat twist.

They stood at a sensual impasse.

At least, that's what it felt like to Matt. He didn't want to move, didn't want to let her out the door.

"Can I have this dance?" she asked, a laugh in her voice.

He suspected that she was joking about them coming face-to-face in the doorway. Or, rather, his gaze to her face.

But for a moment Matt wished that he'd been standing on his own two feet, in full control of his movements.

Because if he had been, he just might have swept her into his arms, danced her back into the house and told her how damn pretty she was.

As it was, maybe it was for the best that he was dumbstruck and unable to say or do something he might regret later.

Chapter Eight

Tori had just left the house and stepped off the front porch when Jared Clayton's dual-wheeled pickup drove into the yard.

Good, she thought. Now all of Granny's sons had arrived. And so had Sabrina, the Rocking C bookkeeper, whose nephew, Joey, was recovering nicely from heart surgery on Jared's ranch.

Since Tori hadn't seen any of them after Joey's discharge from the hospital, she was eager to greet them and catch up on everything.

Jared rolled down his window, and Tori approached the door. As she peered inside the idling vehicle, she saw the six-year-old boy sitting between the adults.

"You're looking great," Tori told Joey. "How are you feeling?"

"I'm good." He grinned. "It was hurting before. But not anymore."

"I'm glad to hear that."

"How is Smokey doing?" the boy asked. "I'll bet he misses me."

Before the surgery, when they'd all been staying on the Rocking C, it hadn't been any secret that the boy loved horses and cowboys. So Jared had asked Joey to look after an old black gelding on his ranch. The child had been thrilled to be granted such a wonderful chore and had taken his job seriously.

"Smokey is doing just fine," Tori told him, "and I'm sure he'll be happy to see you."

"How are the kittens?" the boy asked. "Are they still little?"

"They're doing very well, too." She hated to tell him that the mother cat had died. It hadn't been that long ago when Joey had lost his own mother, and he didn't need the reminder. So if he didn't ask, she wouldn't offer that bit of news. "They were just newborns when you left, so they're bigger now. Matt thinks they're about one month old. Their eyes are open, and they're able to walk around."

"Cool." The boy grinned. "I can't wait to see them."

Tori's gaze shifted to Jared. "Would you mind parking along the road that leads to the pond so Granny won't see your truck when she arrives?"

"No, not at all. Do you really think you've managed to keep this thing a surprise?"

"I believe so." A light summer breeze kicked up a stand of her hair and blew it across her face. She tucked it behind her ear. "But it wasn't easy."

Sabrina opened the passenger door, slid off the seat and waited for Joey to get out. Once the door had been shut, Jared turned the vehicle around and headed down the drive to find another parking spot.

Joey, who'd made his way to Tori, wrapped his arms around her waist and gave her a big hug. "I missed you and everybody else. But do you know what? Jared's ranch is just as fun as this one. He's got horses there, too. And as soon as the doctor says I can ride, he's going to give me more lessons."

"I'm glad." Tori caressed the top of the boy's dark head, glad to know his life would soon be back to normal.

"I'd like to see Pumpkin and Fur Ball," he said. "Are the kitties still in the barn? In the same place?"

"No," Tori said. "They're in a box in my bedroom, next to the dresser. If it's okay with Sabrina, you can go into the house and look at them."

"Can I?" he asked his aunt, eyes wide and hopeful.

Sabrina smiled. "Sure, honey. But just for a minute or two. Granny will be coming soon, and we need to find out where we're supposed to wait so we can surprise her."

"Okay." He spun around and strode toward the house as if he'd never had a heart problem, as if he hadn't had surgery to correct a defective valve a little more than three weeks ago.

"It's great to see him happy and well again," Tori said.

"It sure is."

Tori studied the pretty, dark-haired bookkeeper who had become a friend over the past few months. "You're looking good, too, Sabrina."

"Thanks. I've never been happier." Sabrina slipped an

arm around Tori and gave her a quick hug. "I'm afraid I'm going to have to give Granny my notice, though. I've been offered a better position."

"Are you going to work for Jared?" It had been an easy assumption to make.

Sabrina lifted her left hand, where a shiny new diamond sparkled on her ring finger.

Tori's breath caught. "Oh, Sabrina. It's beautiful! I guess that means your new job description includes being a wife."

"We haven't set a date, but Jared surprised me with the ring last night." Sabrina glanced at the front door, then back at Tori. "While Joey's in the house, I want to ask you something. Do you think Granny would mind if Jared and I left Joey here for a few days to a week?"

"I'm sure she wouldn't. She adores him, and Connie and I would be glad to have him around. What's up?"

"My brother, Carlos, Joey's father, is in prison for a crime he didn't commit. Jared and I hired a private investigator and retained an attorney."

Tori hadn't known that. She and Sabrina had become friends while living at the Rocking C, but they hadn't shared everything, which was understandable. After all, Tori had a few secrets of her own.

"Last night we learned that two new witnesses had been found," Sabrina added. "And they can back up his defense. So there's a good possibility that Carlos may be released. It's a long story, but there's going to be a special hearing, and we want to show family support. We also plan to let the judge know that Jared has a job for Carlos and will let him live on the ranch with us."

"I'm sure your efforts will be helpful."

"That's what we're hoping. Anyway, I don't want to take Joey, yet I'm uneasy leaving him behind." She smiled and gave a little shrug. "But I wouldn't worry about him if he stayed here. You know, with you being a nurse and all."

Tori placed a hand on Sabrina's shoulder. "I'll keep a close eye on him."

"I don't know what we would have done if you hadn't been here that day to pick up on the problem. And besides that, your support before, during and after the surgery was a real godsend."

"You're welcome. I'm glad I was able to help."

When Joey came out the door, grinning from ear to ear and chattering about his kittens, the women let the subject of their discussion drop.

"Is there anything I can do to help with the party?" Sabrina asked.

"I've got everything under control. All we have to do is wait for Granny to arrive."

"When is she coming?" Joey asked.

Tori glanced at her wristwatch. "Uh-oh. Anytime. I'd better get everyone rounded up so we can yell surprise."

They'd no more than headed toward the barn when Jared returned from moving his truck. His gaze wandered toward the corral, where Matt had parked his wheelchair away from all the activity and in the shade of a tree. An older couple had just walked away from Matt when Joey approached the cowboy to say hello.

A frown marred Matt's handsome face, suggesting he wasn't all that happy with the attention.

"I hope my brother hasn't been giving you any trouble," Jared said.

Tori chuckled. "I think Trouble is his middle name. But he's making a lot of progress. He started physical therapy last week and has been using a walker more each day, so that's good."

Jared again stole a peek at his brother. "He doesn't look too happy right now."

"He seems to be in a much better mood when he's in the walker or moving around." Tori studied the ex-rodeo cowboy, her heart going out to him. "I've learned that he doesn't like sympathy or offers of assistance. So I suspect that with all the people stopping by to chat and share their compassion, he feels even more imprisoned by that chair."

"You're probably right," Jared said. "If it wasn't Granny's birthday, I suspect he'd be hanging out inside the house."

"Jared!" Doc Graham, who'd arrived earlier, approached and reached out his hand. As the men greeted each other, Tori left them alone so they could talk.

Minutes later, as everyone had been shepherded into the barn to hide until Granny's return, one of the ranch hands who'd been standing guard down the driveway hollered, "Hey, everybody! She's coming!"

"Shh!" someone said. "Quiet!"

A giggle erupted, then another, but the voices quickly stilled as the sound of an approaching engine sounded. According to plan, Hilda was bringing Granny home early from their usual Sunday outing.

After Hilda parked her Cadillac near the front porch, the women got out of the car.

They hadn't made two steps toward the house when Jared pushed against the barn doors, opening them so

Granny's friends and neighbors could rush out and shout, "Surprise!"

Granny's hand flew to her chest, and her mouth gaped open. "Well, I'll be…" She shot a glance at her friend. "Hilda, did you know about this?"

"Yes, I did. And we were all determined to keep this party a secret since we've never been able to surprise you before."

"Well, you certainly pulled it off." A grin lit up Granny's eyes. "I guess that means you don't need those aspirins after all."

Hilda chuckled. "The headache was an excuse to end our day and bring you home."

"Come on," Jared said. "Let's get this celebration underway."

Tori shot a glance at Matt, whose scowl had softened a tad. Still, something told her this was going to be a long, drawn-out day for him.

For a moment their gazes locked and something passed between them. Something with warmth and substance. Something that gripped her heart and wrung out every bit of emotion that lurked inside.

And she wondered what—if anything—she should do about it.

An hour later the party was in full swing as Tori made her rounds, checking the buffet line they'd set up outdoors, at the back of the barn.

The crew from Chuck's Wagon stood on hand to help serve people, and it looked as though there was still plenty to eat.

Granny and Hilda stood next to the salads, surveying the spread.

"I don't know why you took me to lunch after church," Granny said to her friend. "You know how much I love to eat good barbecue."

Hilda snatched a carrot stick from a platter of vegetables. "You've been telling us all how much you wanted a surprise party, but no one has ever been able to pull it off before. So if I hadn't stopped at Caroline's Diner after church like we do every Sunday, you would have been suspicious and wondered if something else had been planned instead."

Tori grinned as she made her way to the beverage table. She noted that they were getting low on lemonade and iced tea, so she headed for the kitchen for more.

There she found Connie seated at the antique walnut table, an open magazine spread before her.

"Why are you hanging out in here?" she asked.

"No reason."

Connie usually spent a lot of time alone, which Tori supposed was okay. Some people were just naturally reserved, although the new cook seemed to take shyness to the extreme.

"I don't want to press you to do something you don't want to do," Tori said. "I realize some people are uncomfortable in crowds."

"I'm okay with that." Connie closed the magazine she'd been perusing and pushed it aside. "It's just that I prefer to keep a low profile these days."

"You mean you haven't always?"

"Not really."

Tori wanted to quiz her further, but thought better of it. She supposed it wasn't right to pry when she'd taken a break from her own life and preferred to keep her reasons for doing so to herself.

When it appeared that Connie wasn't going to be any more forthcoming, Tori said, "You ought to see all the food that Chuck's Wagon prepared. It probably won't last long. Are you hungry?"

"A little."

"Then why don't you come out with me and get a plate? You can always bring it back in here if you'd rather eat where it's quiet."

Connie seemed to consider that option, then scooted her chair back and stood.

"Will you help me carry something outside?" Tori asked. "It'll keep me from making two trips."

"Sure."

Tori handed Connie the plastic container of lemonade, then grabbed the gallon jug of sweetened sun tea from the counter.

Together, they walked through the living room, out the front door and into the yard. Most of the party guests had moved out back to the tables that had been placed under the shade of the trees, where the caterer was setting out food.

"From what I understand," Tori said, "Greg is going to perform a couple of his songs today. Have you ever heard his music?"

"Yes, I have," Connie said. "He's got a lot of talent, and his career seems to have taken off nicely."

They carried the tea and lemonade to the beverage

table. As Tori replenished the empty pitchers, she encouraged Connie to fill a plate while the food was still out.

After finishing the chore she'd set out to accomplish, Tori placed her hands on her hips and scanned the guests who were either sitting at tables or mingling in small groups.

Matt had parked his wheelchair near the corral. He'd been off by himself most of the day.

Tori had suggested that he not use the walker during the party. The ground was soft and uneven in spots, and she'd been afraid that he'd get tired or have trouble maneuvering it through the crowd. She also feared that he might lose his balance and fall.

He hadn't fought her suggestion. But since he'd begun to use the walker, she'd noted that he seemed to be more withdrawn than usual when using the wheelchair. And she suspected that might be the reason for his deep frown today.

Or it might be the hordes of people who continued to stop by and chat with him. Right this minute, Joey was talking to him.

A furrowed brow marred the handsome cowboy's face, and Tori wondered if the boy was annoying him.

There was only one way to find out. She made her way toward them.

She'd been so wrapped up in party preparations and in being a good hostess that now she realized she hadn't been sensitive to Matt, to his needs or his comfort.

As she approached, she heard Joey say, "We're going to have chocolate cake pretty soon, and I can hardly wait."

"Good," Matt replied. "Maybe you ought to go hang out next to it so you can have the first piece."

"But it's Granny's birthday," Joey argued. "She's supposed to get served first."

"Then maybe you can have the next slice," Matt said. Was he trying to get rid of the sweet little boy?

"Okay," Joey said. "Then I'll wait in line. Do you want me to get you some cake, too? I can bring it back to you."

"No, thanks."

As Joey left, Tori crossed her arms. "Is it my imagination, or did you just run that child off?"

"Hanging out here and badgering me with a million questions isn't going to do him any good."

Was there something in particular Joey had wanted to know? Something that had set Matt off?

"What did he ask you?"

Matt chuffed and gripped the wheels of his chair. "He wanted to know if I'd be able ride in the rodeo again. And he asked how the accident happened. He also wanted to know if anyone else had gotten hurt."

No wonder Matt had bristled and grown solemn.

"Did you tell him?" Tori asked.

"No. Those questions hammer at me constantly, and I have a hard enough time pondering the answers myself."

Tori wanted to wrap her arms around him, to offer him comfort. Understanding. Compassion.

But she didn't dare. For all she knew, he might slip right back into his old frame of mind and recoil from her touch.

Still, there had to be something else she could do to help, something she could say.

"Joey said he's going to stay here for a few days," Matt said, interrupting her thoughts.

"That's right." Tori was already looking forward to

having the little boy around. He loved the ranch, and everything was a new discovery.

But when she glanced down at Matt, when she saw his terse lips, she realized he probably didn't feel the same way she did.

"What's the matter?" she asked.

"Nothing."

Tori didn't buy that for a minute. Joey loved cowboys and idolized Matt because of his rodeo accomplishments. So she would have thought that he would be flattered by the attention of a little hero worship. Yet he clearly wasn't.

"I don't believe you," she said.

Matt shrugged. "It's not the kid. Not really. With everyone feeling obligated to stop and offer their sympathy and everything, I'd like to disappear with a bottle of Jack Daniel's."

"But you haven't done that," Tori said.

"Apparently, I can be a jerk when I drink to excess. And this feels like it could definitely be one of those days. So I'll suffer through all the condolences."

"I'm sorry this afternoon has been a pain for you."

He shrugged. "I owe it to Granny."

If one considered outward appearances, it would seem that Matt was self-centered and simply feeling sorry for himself. But Tori knew that wasn't the case. So she was determined to help, to do something to ease his emotional discomfort. And she was determined to do whatever it took to ease his pain.

"I need to make the rounds again and see that everyone has what they need," she said to excuse herself. "I'll be back."

Then she returned to the center of the party, hoping to come up with an idea that would help Matt feel like a vibrant man again, and convinced that was exactly what he needed.

As Tori continued her job as hostess, she scanned the guests, spotting Jared near the punch table. Since he wasn't chatting with anyone, she decided it was a perfect time to approach him.

"Have you got a minute?" she asked the rancher.

"Sure. What's up?"

Tori nibbled on her bottom lip as she pondered the best way to ask Jared what Joey had wanted to know, a question she had, too. "Will you tell me about Matt's accident? How did it happen?"

Jared lifted his Stetson and raked a hand through his hair, then he adjusted the hat back on his head. "Matt, his fiancée and her four-year-old son had been at a family reunion. On the way home, a couple of drag racers came barreling down the road. Matt veered to the left to avoid them, but he lost control of the vehicle. He blames himself, although the police report said it wasn't his fault."

"That's too bad," Tori said. "He must have loved Cindy a lot."

"I suppose."

Tori picked up on an odd vibe in Jared's answer. "What does that mean?"

"I only met her a time or two, and she seemed nice. But I'm not sure that she was Matt's type."

That was interesting, Tori thought. Jared had made the same comment as Granny had about the woman. "What makes you say that?"

"Matt's strong-willed. And I think he needs a woman

who will stand up to him. Challenge him. And Cindy was pretty soft-spoken and compliant. But that's all water under the bridge now."

"Still, he wouldn't have been engaged to marry her if he hadn't loved her. Sometimes opposites attract."

"I suppose they do."

Jared turned to Tori, his eyes sweeping the length of her. "Actually, Cindy looked a lot like you. Same fair complexion, same hair color. She was a bit taller than you, though. And she wasn't quite as pretty."

For a moment Tori felt inclined to thank him for the compliment, but the fact that she resembled Matt's deceased fiancée made her feel a little uneasy. Surely Matt had noticed, too.

Did that mean it bothered Matt to be around Tori, just as it apparently bothered him to be around Joey?

He and Tori certainly hadn't hit it off at first.

Of course, they'd had some nice moments, especially on those evening walks that had become a habit.

Her thoughts drifted to the trip to Wexler they'd taken for his physical therapy appointment. The day he'd joked about copping a feel.

At that very moment, as he'd caressed her cheek, then slowly allowed his hand to skim her throat and chest, their eyes had locked on each other. And, joke or no joke, something heated had passed through them. Something that made her feel vibrant and alive.

Like a woman who was lovable and deserved to be loved. And for a moment she forgot all about James and her sister.

Maybe there was something therapeutic about facing one's fears, about getting back in the saddle of life again.

"Thanks for your insight," she told Jared. "It helps me understand him better."

"Good luck. Whatever you're doing seems to be working. At least you got him into physical therapy."

Yes, she'd managed to do that.

She started to turn and leave, but caught herself and spun back around. "Oh! Congratulations on your engagement."

"Thanks." A grin lit up his face, reflecting his happiness.

It was uplifting to know that Sabrina and Jared had fallen in love, yet Tori couldn't help wondering if she would ever be that fortunate.

She'd been hopeful once, when she and James had been lovers. But the charming intern and her sister had put an end to that dream, leaving her feeling as though she was lacking what it took to keep a man satisfied.

As she returned to Matt, she realized that they'd both lost a lover, although the circumstances had been different. Still, they were each alone and hurting in their own ways.

He watched her approach, and she couldn't help gazing at him. He was a handsome man—too handsome to spend the rest of his life in solitude, feeling sorry for himself.

"I take it everything is going well and on schedule," he said.

"Yes, just like clockwork."

But some things weren't right. And she felt a growing compulsion to do something about it, although she didn't know what.

Perhaps a heart-to-heart with Matt would help.

More often than not in the past, he'd shrugged off her

attempts to help, even when doing so meant he risked collapsing into a heap on the ground and hurting himself.

Like he'd nearly done after that first physical therapy appointment in Wexler.

Again her mind drifted to the day they'd embraced, hearts beating. The whisper of a touch. The catch of her breath. The heat of his gaze as it locked on hers.

And again she shook it off.

Still, she couldn't let him sit here any longer, punishing himself and feeling miserable.

Should she try to take him aside and talk to him? Over the last week or so, they'd seemed to have forged a friendship of sorts. And he was always more forthcoming when they were alone.

Maybe, if she could walk that fine line between sympathy and understanding, she might be able to pull him out of the doldrums.

Of course, he probably wouldn't agree to it.

But what had Jared said?

Matt's strong-willed. And I think he needs a woman who will stand up to him. Challenge him.

Well, Tori certainly had no problem doing that. So she got behind his wheelchair and began to push.

"Where the hell do you think you're going?" he asked.

"I figured you wouldn't mind if we slipped away from the party for a while."

He didn't respond, so she figured he was game.

Trouble was, she didn't really know what she was going to say to him when she got him alone.

It would come to her, she supposed.

For a moment, as she pushed him around the barn and

toward the side of the house, she had second thoughts about being so assertive, especially without any real game plan. But she pressed on.

When they were alone at the side of the house and there was no chance anyone would come upon them, she slowed his wheelchair to a stop. Then she walked around to the front of the chair.

His brow furrowed and his lips tensed as he waited for her to speak.

It wasn't too late, she reminded herself. She could give him one of those it's-time-to-straighten-up-and-fly-right talks.

His chin lifted, and his hands gripped the sides of his chair, as though he was sorely tempted to stand up and face her challenge—whatever it might be. "Have you got a burr under your saddle?"

"No. Not really." She couldn't blame him for thinking she'd planned a big confrontation. After all, she'd whisked him away from the crowd as though she did. But actually, she'd known how badly he disliked being confined to that chair and at the mercy of those around him.

So now, with no great plan coming to her, she had to think of a way to backpedal.

He eyed her intently as though he was trying to get to the root of her action, and God only knew what he'd uncovered.

Then he sank back in his seat and crossed his arms. "What's on your mind?"

She'd be darned if she even had a suspicion any longer. Not when she was mesmerized by whatever was simmering in his eyes—dark and dangerous. Alluring and arousing.

She recognized it, though. It was the same heated

something that had sent her senses reeling when they'd been in Wexler, when she'd stepped in to help him from falling when he was climbing back into the truck.

And it was doing it to her again, snaking around her heart and threatening to draw her deep inside of him.

Her brains must have just turned to mush, because for the life of her, it seemed as though someone else said, "There's life after grief, Matt."

"What's that supposed to mean?"

Darned if she knew.

"Why'd you drag me away from the barn?" he asked.

"I'm not sure." A whimsical smile settled on her face as she tried to make light of what she'd done, as well as the adolescent urges zinging through her. "Maybe I'd like to cop a feel of my own."

Oh, dear God. Had she said that?

She'd meant it as a joke, as a bridge to span two awkward pauses in the conversation. But the look in his eyes told her he didn't find it the least bit funny.

And that he might even want to hold her to it.

Chapter Nine

Maybe I'd like to cop a feel of my own.

What in the hell had provoked her to say something like that?

And what, exactly, was going on in that pretty little head of hers?

Matt sat back in his chair, rocked to the core—and tempted beyond belief.

Had she been serious?

Either way, she had him intrigued.

Her hair had come loose from its bun, and the breeze whipped a long, curly red tendril across her face. She brushed it away.

Usually he couldn't stand being looked down upon, which was one reason he hated sitting in this chair. Being the only one seated often stirred up images of his drunken uncle standing over him, with his fist and his voice raised. And so that particular position usually made Matt want to lash out, to fight back.

But right this minute, looking up at Tori didn't have the same effect.

As if reading his mind and knowing his secret peeve, she knelt before him and placed a hand on his thigh. "I'm sorry, Matt. That came out badly."

"Actually, it didn't sound so bad to me." He wasn't really sure what she'd been getting at, and although he'd easily made the leap to sex, he didn't want to make any false assumptions.

"I guess I was just trying to lighten things up."

"Well, it worked. And I don't think you were joking. Not completely."

"Okay," she said. "I'll admit it. I find you attractive. And it's been a long time since…"

"Since you've had sex?"

Her cheeks flushed a deep shade of red. "Okay. So I made a joke that could be taken…"

"Seriously?" he asked. Because he could certainly take it that way.

"Stop trying to put words in my mouth."

"You started it."

"No, you did. That day in Wexler." She blew out a sigh. "The one and only guy I ever got involved with found someone he liked better than me. So I decided to steer clear of men for a while."

"Then maybe it's time you got back in the saddle again."

"You might be right." The hint of a smile—one part shy, two parts naughty—sparked a glimmer in her eyes.

There had to be a hundred reasons why Matt and Tori shouldn't get physically involved—if that's what they were tiptoeing around—yet he'd be damned if he could think of a single one.

Instead he imagined the two of them lying naked in bed, hands touching, exploring. Caressing each other.

Just the thought was enough to chase away the reverberating sounds of clucking tongues and the condolences Granny's friends and neighbors had been drowning him with for the past couple of hours or so.

Their well-intentioned sympathy had only served to stir up his frustration and the guilt he'd been carrying since the accident, but he no longer cared about that now.

Tori touched his cheek, and he found the press of her fingers to be a balm—and far more of one than the compassion he'd been bathed in earlier today.

"You had a tough break, Matt. But your life isn't over. And neither is mine."

As much as he'd wanted to hear her voice the words, he made the leap for them both. "Are we skating around the idea of making love, or are we ready to jump right in?"

She swallowed, a shy smile chasing away all signs of the naughty one. "I don't know. I guess it depends."

"On what?"

"On whether you're interested or not."

He shouldn't be.

But he was.

He placed his hand along the side of her throat, his fingers sliding under a cascade of curls. He used his thumb to caress her cheek. "I'm definitely interested.

And for the record, my legs are the only things giving me any trouble. So if you'd like to give the rest of me a workout, I'm game."

"I really didn't have a motive for coming out here with you—other than to offer you a bit of an escape and to…" She gave a little shrug. "Oh, I don't know."

"Maybe, deep inside, you *do*."

He released his hold, letting his knuckles brush along her throat and down her chest.

But this time, his hand skimmed over her breast, then lingered. He felt the fullness, the softness, the warmth. His thumb grazed her nipple, which hardened in response.

Her breath caught, and her lips parted. When she finally spoke, her voice came out husky and whisper soft. "I've got to put candles on the cake."

She was certainly the right person for that job. She'd just lit a fire under him.

Before she could stand and get behind his wheelchair, Joey came around the corner. "Oh, there you are, Tori. I've been looking all over for you. What are you doing way over here?"

"I was just…talking to Matt."

"But all the fun is over near the barn."

"It was kind of fun over here." Matt's gaze lit on Tori, and he tossed her a grin.

He hoped they weren't tiptoeing on something they shouldn't be messing with.

Things could get…sticky, if they weren't careful.

But Matt had always been up for a challenge.

* * *

The conversation he'd had with Tori at the side of the house continued to replay itself over and over in Matt's mind, even after they'd returned to the party.

Were they really skating around the idea of an affair?

The more he thought about it, the more appealing the idea was.

Trouble was, with a house full of people, it was going to be tough finding some privacy. But Matt had always been innovative—when he'd had reason to be.

As he sat parked in the shade of the sycamore, he watched as Tori called everyone to the dessert table. Then she placed eight candles on the birthday cake—one for each decade of Granny's life—and lit them.

After Greg led a round of "Happy Birthday," Granny made a wish and blew out the candles amidst the cheers and the applause of her friends.

"It's time to open presents," Tori said, as she pulled out a chair for Granny and stacked the gifts next to her.

As Granny oohed and ahhed over each item she'd been given—a box of chocolates, a basket of soap and lotions, a new sweater, a pair of slippers and more, Matt's gaze again drifted to Tori, where she stood near the table that held one of the cakes Connie had baked. She was cutting slices and placing them on small paper plates.

Each time she glanced up from her work, their eyes met, letting him know that she'd been thinking about him, too.

Was she having second thoughts?

A blush on her cheeks suggested she might be.

As Greg began to strum the chords of his guitar, Matt turned his attention to his brother and listened as the singer launched into several of his biggest hits, much to the delight of all the guests.

Even Connie swayed to the music, although she stood off by herself—much like Matt tried to do these days.

One nice thing was that the party was almost over, and they'd both soon be free to go about their business.

After everyone had been served cake, Tori brought Matt a slice, along with a fork and paper napkin.

He took it from her, noting she'd given him an extra large piece. "Thanks. I hope we still have some of that chocolate cake left."

"There ought to be plenty leftover." She crossed her arms and shifted her weight to one hip.

"You've got to be tired," he said. "I haven't seen you stop all day."

Except, of course, when she'd taken him to the side of the house and knelt in front of him.

She blew out a weary sigh. "To be honest, I'm looking forward to putting my feet up."

"Have you had a chance to eat yet?" he asked.

"Cake?"

"I was thinking about lunch. You've been trying so hard to take care of everyone else that I'm afraid you might not have taken time for yourself."

Her lips parted, and a whisper of surprise crossed her face. "Actually, I planned to eat later. After everyone else…"

Matt reached for her hand. His thumb grazed her wrist, where her pulse throbbed. He could swear it was going haywire. "Is that the nurse in you talking?"

"I'm not sure I know what you mean."

He slowly released her wrist. "You've been fussing

about everyone but yourself. And I have a feeling that's the norm for you."

"You're the first one who's ever called me on that."

That was too bad. It should have been clear to anyone who knew her. "Why don't you go fix yourself a plate? I'll have Lester ask some of the hands to clean up whatever the caterer leaves behind."

"Thanks. I'd appreciate that." She blew out a breath. "I'll be glad when this party winds down."

So would Matt. He was eager to slip away and find some peace and quiet—hopefully with Tori. That way, they could finish that little talk they'd started, the one Joey had interrupted.

Of course, even after everyone went home, he and Tori would be hard-pressed to find any privacy.

There was always Clem's cabin, he supposed. When Sabrina had been here, she'd planned to move into it and had cleaned it up. But after talking to Jared today, Matt had realized that Sabrina wouldn't be coming back to the Rocking C to live.

That wouldn't leave Granny in a lurch, though. Jared had asked Matt to continue doing the bookwork until Granny was able to hire someone else.

Still, that was quite a trek to the little cabin on the knoll. And at this point, neither the wheelchair nor the walker was likely to make it.

Damn. He'd have to figure out something else. He drummed his fingers on the sidebar of the wheelchair as he considered other options.

Once, when he'd been a teenager, he'd sneaked

Bonnie Sue Riley into the hay loft. But since his legs were still healing, he wasn't going to be able to make that climb right now.

"Well, look here," Granny said, as she approached. "Just the two I wanted to see."

"Do you need something?" Tori asked.

"Nope." Granny grinned. "I just wanted to thank you both for planning this wonderful party. You have no idea how touched I am."

"Tori's the one who did all the work," Matt said.

Before either Tori or Granny could respond, Greg joined them. "I've got to be taking off, Granny."

"I understand," their mother said. "I'm thrilled that you were able to make it, especially when you've been so busy."

"I wouldn't have missed it." Greg glanced down at the plate Matt held. "Hey, eat up, brother. That chocolate cake was the best I've ever eaten."

Granny smiled proudly. "Connie made it. She's my new cook."

"Lucky you," Greg said. "I get stuck eating most of my meals out."

Matt nearly choked, but he held his tongue. He supposed there wasn't any need to complain about the crummy meals Connie fixed.

"Joe's waiting in the car for me, so I better go." Greg gave their mother a big hug, holding her a bit longer than usual.

But Matt understood why. His brother loved Granny every bit as much as he and Jared did.

When the embrace finally ended, Greg added, "I'm

going to be traveling a lot in the next few months, so I'm not sure when I'll get to see you again. But I'll definitely be home for Thanksgiving. I told my manager not to book anything until after the new year."

"That's wonderful." Granny clapped her hands. "How long can you stay?"

"At least a month. Maybe longer."

"That's the best news I've had in ages. I'll have all my boys home for the holidays." Granny's happiness lit up her face and made her look ten years younger.

"Now, don't go to any extra work for me," Greg said, his voice growing stern. "I don't want you worrying about cooking or baking. I'd rather you relaxed and enjoyed our time together."

"Don't worry," Granny said. "I won't do too much. I've got a cook, remember? So there'll be plenty in the way of food. Maybe we can even fatten you up while you're here. All that traveling from city to city is taking a toll on you. You're too skinny, son."

"Maybe so." Greg chuckled. "But if Connie's cooking is as good as her baking, I'm sure I'll be as plump as a Christmas goose by New Year's Eve."

Uh-oh, Matt thought. If his younger brother was looking forward to Connie's meals, he was going to be in for a big surprise. Of course, maybe Connie would learn to cook by then. Otherwise, Matt was going to suggest that Tori prepare the holiday meals—or at least take an active part.

Greg, with the strap of his guitar slung over his shoulder, said goodbye and took off to meet Joe in the car.

"By the way," Granny said. "I'm going to look after Joey for a few days. Isn't that nice?"

"Yep." Matt tried to feign a little enthusiasm.

To be honest, he hadn't been happy to hear that the six-year-old would be staying at the ranch for a while. But not because he didn't like kids. Or even *that* particular kid.

It's just that Tommy used to look at him with those same soulful brown eyes. Eyes that suggested Matt could do no wrong. And Matt knew better than to be swept away by undeserved hero worship. So he would just try to keep his distance, although that might be a lot easier said than done. For some reason, Joey seemed to gravitate toward him.

"You know," Granny said to Tori. "I think I'll take Joey shopping in Houston tomorrow. Sabrina said that he'll be starting first grade soon, so I figure he'll need some new clothes, a backpack and other supplies. I used to enjoy getting ready for each new school year. It'll be a nice outing. In fact, maybe we'll pack a suitcase and make it an overnight trip."

"Do you want me to go with you?" Tori asked.

"No, someone needs to stay and cook for the men. And since Connie's pants are getting snug in the waist, I'll take her with me. I'd like to surprise her with some maternity clothes."

"I'm sure Joey will do fine," Tori said, "but maybe you ought to run that by Sabrina first."

"I will. But I'll remind her that we'll be close to the hospital and his doctors in Houston, just in case something happens."

"I'm sure you won't have to worry about that," Tori said.

Perfect, Matt thought. If Granny, Joey and Connie were leaving for an overnight shopping trip, then he and Tori would be left alone at the house.

He settled back into his chair and grinned.

Finding some privacy wasn't going to be as hard as he'd thought.

After the party Tori had been tired, but she hadn't realized just how much.

Once back in the house she'd fed the kittens, then kicked off her shoes, slipped off her dress and had lain down on the top of the bed for a little nap. The next thing she knew it was morning.

As she readied for the day, she thought about the sexually charged conversation she'd had with Matt yesterday. She hadn't meant to agree to have an affair, but they'd certainly touched on the subject.

Touched.

When Matt's hand had grazed her breast, her nipple contracted in response to the intimate caress, flooding her with desire. And her body—deep within her feminine core—had reawakened.

For the first time since she'd told James to get out of her life, she'd felt desirable again. And she'd wondered if there was a chance that making love would do both her and Matt some good.

But could she go through with it? Could she have a no-strings-attached affair?

She wasn't sure.

Tori kept busy until after ten, when Granny rounded up Joey and Connie and herded them out to one of the ranch vehicles. Connie had been reluctant to go into town, but she got behind the wheel. Minutes later they were gone.

Earlier, Matt had disappeared into the office, so Tori prepared lunch for the men—leftovers from yesterday.

It wasn't until late afternoon when Matt came into the kitchen and fixed himself a barbecue beef sandwich. "What's for dinner tonight?"

"I thought I'd make pork chops. Is that all right with you?"

"Sure."

Several minutes of silence followed, and when Tori couldn't stand it any longer, she asked, "Are we going to talk about yesterday?"

"You mean the party?"

Did she have to spell it out for him?

"No, I was thinking that we might want to discuss that little chat we had." And the intimate way he'd touched her. The unspoken words that had passed between them. The urges he'd stirred up inside of her.

"You're not backing out, are you?"

Her pulse stopped, then spiked. "Backing out of what? We didn't exactly decide to move forward on anything."

"Didn't we?"

She stole a glance at him, watched him studying her in a way that made her feel as though she'd left the house half dressed. "I wasn't suggesting that we…you know."

"Sleep together?" he asked.

"I mean, if you don't want to—"

"Hey. When a beautiful woman suggests sex, a man would have to be crazy to not be interested."

"I'm not that kind of woman."

"You mean, beautiful?"

She slapped her hands on her hips. "That's not what I

meant. But no, I don't see myself as beautiful. And I don't believe in sex without a commitment. But in this case, I thought…"

"You thought what?" His brow furrowed, yet his lips quirked in a smile.

Darn. The man was infuriating. She suspected he was playing with her—and enjoying it.

"I agreed that I was…thrown from a horse—so to speak."

"Are we still talking about sex?"

She knit her brow and shot him a look of exasperation. *"Yes."*

He wore a cocky grin. Or maybe it was just one of those I-was-funnin'-with-you looks; she couldn't be sure. Either way, the subject seemed to appeal to him.

She was afraid to steal another peek at him, so she got up and reached into the cupboard for a glass. "Anyway, I though it might be good to…you know, get back in the saddle."

There. She'd said it, utilizing the cowboy analogy he'd used yesterday.

"What are you suggesting?" he asked.

"I'm not exactly sure." She poured herself a glass of lemonade. "Remember how I told you that I dated a guy who cheated on me?"

"Yeah. And between you, me and the fence post, the guy didn't deserve a woman like you."

"Maybe not." She worried her bottom lip. "But there's a part of me that wonders if… Well, if maybe it was my fault. If maybe…"

"Don't blame yourself, Tori. Some men are immature jerks when it comes to that sort of thing. When I first started out on the circuit, I used to date several women at the same time. But it wasn't a secret. I was always up front with them, and they had the option of seeing me under those terms."

She supposed it was only fair, although if Matt was seeing someone else, she wouldn't get involved with him.

But this was different, wasn't it?

He wasn't engaged any longer. And he certainly wasn't dating anyone else. They were both adults and able to have a brief, therapeutic sexual fling if they wanted to.

"I realize this wouldn't be anything long-term," she said.

"Good."

She took a sip of lemonade, felt the cool, bittersweet taste as it filled her mouth and tried to wrap her mind around the sexual business deal taking place. "Then I guess we're on the same page."

"Looks like it." He got up from the table. Reaching for the cane he'd leaned against one of the chairs, he got to his feet. "I'm going back into the office. Let me know when dinner's ready."

And that was that.

When Matt left the room, she breaded pork chops and put them in the oven to bake. Then she peeled the potatoes. While she waited for them to come to a boil, she prepared a tossed salad.

Dessert would be something light and easy—ice cream.

But then what? she asked herself.

She'd only had one other sexual partner, and at the time, she'd thought that they'd had something special. That they'd had a future together.

Could she enter a casual sexual relationship with Matt?

Sex always changed things between a couple.

You're not backing out, are you? The question Matt had asked her earlier hung in the air.

She tried to tell herself that she was a nurse, a professional. And that she could be clinical and objective about all of this. Making love with Matt just might right both of their worlds again.

But she couldn't deny that she was having second thoughts. She firmly believed sex wasn't something she could enter into lightly. She'd have to care about the man she slept with.

She had, of course, grown to care about Matt.

Maybe she'd just have to take it one sweet touch at a time.

Chapter Ten

That evening, after Tori called the ranch hands into the kitchen and laid the food she'd fixed on the table, they all raved about the taste of the pork chops, salad, green beans, mashed potatoes and gravy.

And Matt had to agree with them.

"You're one heck of a cook," Lester told Tori.

"That's right," one of the other hands said. "We're lucky to have two great meals in a row."

"Thank you." A light flush tinged Tori's cheeks, making her look especially pretty tonight, even wearing an apron over a pair of jeans and a plain cotton blouse.

"Yeah," Earl, one of the older, weathered cowboys added. "We don't know why Connie's doing all the cooking and you're not."

"I'm sure Granny has her reasons," Tori said. "Besides,

Connie tries hard. And when it comes to whipping up desserts, I can't hold a candle to her."

"That don't matter," Lester said. "Ice cream is fine with us."

Matt figured the men had all been doubling up on dessert for so long that the sweets had lost some of their appeal, but he held his tongue.

Well, at least he kept quiet until the men went back to the bunkhouse and finally left him and Tori alone.

"How are the kittens doing?" he asked.

She turned away from the sink, a damp dishcloth dangling from her hand, and flashed him a smile. "They're doing really well. Even Tippy. I fed them earlier, and I was going to ask if you thought I should start them on a little solid food."

"It probably wouldn't hurt," he said, watching as she went back to rinsing the plates and stacking them in the dishwasher.

He wished he could offer to help her clean up the after-dinner mess in the kitchen, but he wasn't very steady on his feet these days and would probably just get in the way.

More than ever, he was determined to heal and get his body back, even if he wouldn't ever be able to ride competitively again. He figured he'd stewed in his sorrow long enough. What's done was done. It was time to put the past aside—if he could.

He watched as Tori spooned the leftovers into plastic containers then placed them in the refrigerator.

Next, she wiped down the table, the stove and the counters. If he couldn't help, he should at least keep her company.

"Are you up for a walk tonight?" He hoped she'd say yes. He'd actually been looking forward to their time together in the evenings. There'd been something comforting about being alone with her in the moonlight and under a scatter of stars. Something special.

"Sure." She glanced over her shoulder and blessed him with another dimpled smile. "I've just about got the kitchen back in order."

"Good. I want to try this out tonight."

She turned completely, facing him, and leaned her hip against the countertop. Her brow furrowed, and she tucked a long, curly strand of hair behind her ear. "Try out what?"

He lifted the cane he'd found while searching for something else in the office closet. "This used to belong to Everett. I hadn't seen it since the time Granny suggested Greg use it as part of his Halloween costume."

"Who's Everett?" she asked.

"Granny's late husband. He passed away before my brothers and I moved in, so we never got a chance to meet him. I heard he was a true cowboy, the last of a dying breed."

"Why did he need the cane?"

"He had a couple of strokes before suffering a massive heart attack that killed him. So he'd had a bum leg for a while."

Tori rinsed the dishcloth and wrung it out. Then she carefully draped it over the faucet and turned to face him. "I'm really proud of you, Matt."

For a moment, something warm and tingly swelled inside of him, but he shoved it aside as quickly as it surfaced. He hadn't done squat to make anyone proud lately.

"Why would you say that?" he asked.

"Because you're trying so hard."

To walk?

To heal?

To have a better attitude?

Again, he tried to shrug off her comment. "Once I make my mind up to do something, I always try hard. It's the competitor in me."

Still, the sincerity in her tone and her expression—whether deserved or not—touched him in a nice yet unexpected way.

Other than Granny and her old foreman, Clem Bixby, no one had ever told Matt they were proud of him. So he supposed he was a real sucker when it came to hearing the words.

Especially from her.

There was something about Tori that appealed to him. Something none of the other women he'd dated had. Hell, not even Cindy.

He wouldn't ponder what it was, though. Or why it seemed to matter.

Not tonight.

Tori bent to reach for the box of soap that was under the sink, flashing him a lovely view of her perfectly shaped…derriere. For some reason referring to it as an ass seemed crude, even to a man who'd used that term in the past.

Damn. What kind of spell had she cast on him?

Or was it merely the vulnerable position he'd found himself in following the accident?

After she started the washer, she rinsed her hands and reached for a paper towel.

"Are you ready?" she asked, dropping the disposable towel into the trash.

"Yep." He stood and grabbed the cane.

Minutes later they'd made their way outside and were striding toward the barn, slowly but surely. He suspected this walk would end sooner than the rest of them had. He'd probably jumped the gun by choosing to walk with a cane rather than the walker. But what the hell. When he got too sore or tired of walking, he would just suggest that they head back to the porch and sit for a while.

As he leaned upon the cane to move forward step by step, he glanced up at the sky, which was especially clear tonight. The moon was waxing and would soon be full again.

In the corral close to the barn, the chestnut broodmare whinnied, then plodded toward the railing as if she was lonely and in need of a friend.

"What's the matter?" he asked the horse as he started toward the fence. "Do you want some attention?"

Tori followed beside him. "She's a pretty horse. What's her name?"

"Aquila. She was bred to one of the top cutting horses in the state, so we're all excited about her foal." Matt leaned his cane against the fence post, then stroked the mare's neck.

"When is she due?"

"I'm not sure. In a couple of weeks, I think."

Aquila jerked up her head, bumping Matt and knocking him off balance.

Damn. He reached for the railing, just as Tori reached for him.

"Are you okay?" she asked.

"Yeah." At least, he had been until she wrapped her arms around him, until her breasts pressed against his diaphragm. Until her soft floral scent snaked around him, shooting off a surge of testosterone and sending his blood pumping.

As their gazes locked, Matt lost all conscious thought and succumbed to temptation, lowering his mouth for a kiss.

His lips brushed hers once, twice, and he was soon caught up in a swirl of heat and desire.

The kiss intensified, and he leaned against the fence, hoping he wouldn't lose his balance, hoping his aching legs wouldn't buckle. As their tongues caressed, their breaths mingled until they were both consumed by the lust-charged air between them.

Matt couldn't seem to get enough of her, and he lost himself in her wet, velvety mouth. As the kiss deepened, as she tightened her arms around him and pressed her hips against his erection, a shiver of heat slid through his bloodstream, rocking him to the core.

This wasn't going to work. Not here. And not for very much longer.

They would need to move into the privacy of the house, where he could stretch out beside her on a bed and not be hampered by legs that couldn't do all he demanded of them.

He broke the kiss long enough to catch his breath, yet he didn't let go of her; he couldn't.

"As much as I like being outside with you, Tori, I'm going to like being behind closed doors a whole lot more."

"I think I'd like that, too." The arm that she'd wrapped around his waist loosened, and the one that had been around his neck dropped to his chest, her fingers undoubtedly picking up the steady, pounding beat of his heart.

"Do you need help?" she asked. "Should I get the wheelchair?"

"No. It's important for me to make it back to the house on my own."

"But what if you fall?"

It didn't matter.

Sometimes all a man had left was his pride.

Tori had thought long and hard about making love with Matt and had actually decided to go ahead and give it a whirl. But that was before she'd realized how strong her physical response to his kiss had been and how badly she wanted to let herself go. So the closer she got to the house, the more she began to backpedal on that decision.

There was still a big part of her that believed in true love, that clung to an old-fashioned sense of values that insisted sex was something special, something that bound a couple together forever.

And even though she'd come to the conclusion that she had feelings for Matt, she wasn't sure what they were.

What if she actually fell in love with him?

Getting sexually involved with a man who still loved his deceased fiancée wasn't a good idea. Not if Tori wanted to keep her heart intact.

Once they'd returned to the house, Tori led the way to the family room, where she grabbed the television remote and turned on the power. Then she searched the cabinet that held movies until she found the DVD she'd been looking for. She needed time to think before things went further.

"You want to watch TV?" he asked, setting the cane

against the lamp table and plopping down on the sofa. "Forgive me for not sharing your enthusiasm when we could be doing something a lot more fun."

"Believe it or not, there are parts of me that are complaining, too." She held up the movie Sabrina had said was exceptionally good. "But this is a comedy, so it'll be fun."

"It's a chick flick."

"You say that like it's a bad thing." She placed her hands on her hips. "Would you like me to choose a film in which someone dies?"

Matt stiffened, obviously thinking about Cindy and her son.

Oh, God. Why was it such a struggle to say the right thing around him?

"I'm sorry, Matt." She sat next to him on the sofa. "That just slipped out."

He turned to his right, his knee brushing hers. He lifted his hand and trailed his knuckles along her cheek. "I know. Don't worry about it. There's life after grief, remember?"

Yes, she'd told him that. And she desperately wanted to believe it—at least for his sake.

Her heart surged with compassion—or was it something else? She couldn't be sure, but whatever it was filled her chest to the brim.

Their gazes met and locked.

Matt reached for the back of her head and slowly pulled her mouth toward his.

Oh, God. He was going to kiss her again.

Every bit of sense she'd ever had told her to pull back, to put a stop to what would surely be an arousing assault of her senses.

No, her conscience tried to say, yet it didn't do any good. Tori couldn't stop herself.

The kiss began softly, tentatively, just as the last one had.

Her lips parted of their own accord, and his tongue swept inside her mouth as though it belonged there, as though it had come home to stay. Kissing Matt felt good—and right—sparking something deep inside her and triggering thoughts of white lace and forever.

As they necked on the sofa like a couple of teenagers with their hormones raging, she couldn't help wondering if she'd found someone she'd always been looking for, that special something she'd never had.

The idea was both frightening and thrilling.

Yet she couldn't put a stop to the heated assault on her senses. Nor could she keep from leaning into him as he stretched further back against the armrest of the sofa, drawing her to him.

Their hands groped and stroked and touched as though they could somehow get a grip on the desire that raged between them. But control was beyond reach. The need that had been building inside of her exploded, causing an aching emptiness deep in the most feminine part of her.

An emptiness only Matt could fill.

Any thoughts of slowing down had vanished within the inferno of their kisses, but she stopped long enough to catch her breath and say, "Let's go into the bedroom."

"Good idea."

Had she actually suggested that? And would she really be able to go through with it?

Apparently so, because she led him down the hall toward the room she slept in.

Was she somehow overstepping her boundaries as a nurse by having sex with a patient?

No. Matt Clayton was a man, not her patient.

And there was nothing clinical about any of this.

If her heart became involved, as she feared it might— as she feared it actually had—she'd deal with it in the morning. When she'd had her fill of the rugged cowboy.

He pulled on her hand, slowing her steps to a stop.

Was *he* having second thoughts?

She could certainly see the wisdom in refraining from sex and would probably thank him for his foresight later, but she couldn't stop the disappointment from raining down on her.

"I've got some condoms in my room," he said. "Maybe we ought to use that bed."

At this point, with her desire for him raging, she wouldn't complain if they stopped right here and made love on the hall floor, so she allowed him to lead the way.

Once inside his bedroom, she scanned the decor, the oak furniture, the queen-size bed, the blue plaid comforter. She'd cleaned this room many times, yet right now she'd never been more aware of Matt's scent, of his presence.

He took a seat on the edge of the mattress, resting his legs, no doubt. "Come here."

She couldn't have remained in the doorway if she'd wanted to. So she closed the gap between them.

As she neared the bed, he spread his legs so she could get as close to him as possible. As she stood before him, the outsides of her legs touching the insides of his, he reached up and pulled one of her curls, watching as it lengthened then sprang back in place.

"I like your hair. The color, the style."

"Thanks."

Did he like *her,* too? Was there something he saw within her that was different from Cindy? Something that gave Tori a unique place in his… Well, maybe his heart was too much to ask for. But certainly in his thoughts. Was it too much to hope for?

For a moment she wanted to pull away. To insist that he should care for her, too. That whatever she was beginning to feel for him should be mutual.

But she feared they'd moved beyond that now.

So in spite of a momentary hesitation, she chose to not dwell on it.

He placed his hand upon her jaw and drew her lips to his. Within a heartbeat, they were kissing again, deeply, mindlessly. Desperately.

His hands caressed her back, her sides. Up, down and back up again until he sought her breasts and found them ready and practically begging for his touch.

As his thumbs stroked her nipples through the cotton of her shirt and the satin of her bra, her whimper burst forth in his mouth.

Had anything ever felt so good, so arousing?

She wanted to remove her clothes, to feel his skin against hers.

And she wasn't able to wait a minute more.

So she drew back from him long enough to remove her blouse. And as she did so, her eyes locked on his, awaiting his reaction. His response.

She'd give anything to know what he was thinking, what he was feeling.

* * *

Matt watched in awe as Tori lifted her shirt over her head, then dropped it onto the floor. His hormones raged as she unhooked her bra and freed two perfect breasts with their dusky pink nipples contracted in response to their recent foreplay.

A flush blazed across her throat and chest, telling him that her desire for him was every bit as strong as his was for her.

For some reason he suspected that Tori was different from any of the other women he'd known. But he'd be damned if he knew why.

He cupped her face, brushed a thumb across the silky texture of her cheek, saw the glaze of passion in those pretty green eyes. "I'm going to make this special for you, honey."

Oops. Matt didn't use terms of endearments when talking to women, so he wasn't sure where the "honey" had come from. But it no longer seemed to matter when she unbuttoned her pants and pulled down on the zipper. Then she peeled the denim over her hips and stepped out of her jeans altogether.

As he watched her remove her panties—a skimpy white pair—he wanted to shed his clothes, as well. But he was afraid to take his eyes off her, afraid he'd miss the pleasure of all she was offering him.

When she stood before him in naked beauty, he couldn't stand it any longer and peeled off his shirt. Then he drew her into his embrace, relishing the way her breasts splayed against his chest.

Damn, she felt good in his arms.

"I want to make love with you, Matt." Then she pressed

her mouth to his, kissing him senseless and stoking a blaze deep within.

He'd never completely allowed himself to succumb to a woman's allure before, never expected to. And he had the urgent need to bury himself deep inside of Tori, to make her his, if only for tonight.

So he stopped kissing her long enough to shuck off his pants and boxers, then he stretched out on the bed and waited as she joined him.

As they lay side by side, hands seeking and exploring, they made out like a couple who'd saved themselves for each other. A couple who'd never experienced anything like this before.

Odd, he though, shaking off the romantic notion and clinging to the lust that drew him to her.

As their kisses deepened, he was completely swept away. His legs wouldn't allow him to get up on his knees, but it didn't seem to matter. As their lovemaking progressed, he was surprised to find out just how adaptable he was.

Even the occasional ache or pain didn't bother him. And before long, the only thing he was aware of was the heat of her touch, the sweet taste of her mouth, the seductive swirl of her floral scent.

Be careful, a small voice whispered. *Don't get too involved.*

The warning held merit, but right now he didn't care about tomorrow. He just wanted to be deep inside of her, thrusting in and out, taking and giving. Showing her all that making love could be.

He might be sorry later, but he wouldn't worry about

that now. Not when the only thing he could think of doing was to make her writhe with need.

A need only he could fulfill.

As he rolled to the side, taking her with him, she pressed her body against him. Fully aroused, she began to move against his demanding erection, dipping and rubbing and grinding until he thought he'd explode.

"Damn," he said, as he realized that she was the one driving him wild, rather than the other way around.

"Am I hurting you?" she asked, slowing her movements.

Not in the way she thought. But the ache in his loins was begging for release. "I've never been better. And the only thing that's going to hurt me is if you stop doing that."

She smiled, basking in her feminine power, it seemed. Then she proceeded to kiss his jaw, his neck, his chest, his abs, his belly, his…

Good grief, the woman was going to drive him insane.

Before long, they were stroking and caressing and tasting each other, caught up in a fire that might never burn out.

He fumbled for his shaving kit, which rested on the nightstand near the bed and nearly knocked it to the floor. Moments later he came up with a condom. She waited as he ripped into the packet and protected them both.

Finally.

Yet he was torn between wanting to end the sweet aching ecstasy and making it last.

"Would it be better if I got on top?" she asked.

"I don't know about *better*. But it certainly sounds appealing to me." He shot her a grin, thinking it might be nice to let her take the lead.

As he rolled onto his back, she positioned herself over

him. Then, with one knee on each side of his hips, she controlled their initial joining. As she lowered herself, he arched up, and they were soon lost in a lover's frenzy of lust and passion.

Their positions changed several times, and when they peaked, she cried out in pleasure. A powerful climax, the likes of which he'd never had before, damn near turned him inside out, shaking him to the core.

Tori gripped Matt's shoulders and held on tight as she rode each wave of rapture, afraid to open her eyes or breathe.

Their joining had been sweeter and better than she could have imagined, and that left her a bit uneasy.

She'd wanted to make love for the sake of having sex, but she feared it had been so much more than that. At least, it had been to her. She had no idea what to expect when they both came to their senses, but for the time being, she would hold Matt until the last wave of sexual bliss ebbed.

Yet even then she was reluctant to release him, to risk losing what they'd just shared.

Because maybe, if she lay with him long enough, she'd understand why she so desperately wanted to say, "I love you."

It was only sex, she reminded herself. And the overwhelming urge to put a name on what she was feeling and share that emotion with him was merely biological. An innate need to bond.

But she couldn't shake the fear that whatever Matt had stirred up inside her was more than chemistry, more than hormones.

Heaven help her, but somewhere between that first

kiss and the last, she feared that she might have fallen in love with Matt Clayton.

And she wasn't sure what that meant. Because if it was love, she feared it would lead to heartbreak.

After all, there was no way Tori could—or would—compete with a ghost.

Chapter Eleven

The next morning, while Matt sat in the office and went over a bid to repair the roof on one of the outbuildings, his mind kept drifting back to last night. As he relived the pleasures he and Tori had shared in bed, he realized that he finally felt alive again.

He and Tori had made love several times during the night, and at dawn they'd awakened in each other's arms. When Tori glanced at the clock on the bureau and saw the time, she'd quickly excused herself to shower and to make breakfast for the ranch hands.

And, oddly enough, when she'd left Matt in bed, he'd felt a bit…unbalanced.

They'd both known that their affair wouldn't be long-term—which, by the way, was okay with him. But as he lay alone in bed, as he heard the water in the shower turn on, he had to admit that he wasn't ready for it to end. At least, not yet.

He didn't say anything, though.

How could he when they'd both agreed that all they wanted was the physical release that came with sex?

Besides, he wasn't sure what more he wanted from her anyway.

In the past—before Cindy—he hadn't wanted a lasting relationship with anyone.

And after Cindy? Well, he hadn't thought that he would ever want to make that kind of commitment with anyone else again.

But last night, after each heart-spinning climax, when he'd actually had a legitimate reason to roll over and go to sleep, he hadn't. Instead he'd succumbed to the overwhelming compulsion to hold Tori close, to nuzzle her shoulder, to savor the scent of her shampoo.

So what was with that?

For some crazy reason, he hadn't been able to call it a night.

And he still wouldn't.

He blamed that unsettling fact on the accident, on his need to feel whole again. After all, he didn't have anything to offer a woman. Hell, he hadn't even had anything to offer Cindy. He suspected that their relationship had been…

Damn.

He raked his hand through his hair. Whenever his thoughts strayed in that direction, whenever he stirred up the guilt he'd been harboring, his mood floundered.

On the upside, that bit of reality would allow him to roll over and call it a night—figuratively speaking, of course.

So after a morning shower, he'd joined the ranch hands in the kitchen for a breakfast of scrambled eggs, bacon and fried potatoes.

The men had all clucked and fussed over Tori and her cooking skills like little speckled hens, but Matt continued to hold his coffee mug with two hands and pretended to enjoy the flavor of the fresh brew. He'd be damned if he wanted any of those cowboys to suspect what he and Tori had done last night.

As Lester and the others headed outside to start the day, Matt went into the office and got to work.

There was no need to hang around Tori this morning like a lovesick puppy. Besides, he didn't want to lay himself open for one of those awkward, after-the-loving chats, although they'd both been up-front with each other and clear about their expectations. Or, rather, their lack thereof.

Still, making love with her wasn't something he'd easily forget. In fact, just thinking about it slapped a goofy grin on his face.

At just after ten o'clock, a knock sounded on the office door.

"Come on in." He figured it was Tori, but he glanced up to see Lester instead.

Surprisingly, he had to bite back a sense of disappointment.

Lester carried in a stack of envelopes and set them on the desk. "I was at the feed store earlier today, so I stopped by the post office box and picked this up."

"Thanks."

As the ranch foreman left the office, Matt thumbed through the mail, sorting it.

Earl, one of the cowboys who'd worked on the ranch for ages, had gotten a letter from his son in Arkansas.

The bank statement came, as well as the power bill. And Granny had received two birthday cards from friends who hadn't been able to attend the party.

As he neared the bottom of the stack, he spotted another envelope for Tori. And just like the last one, it was from her brother, Sean, who was still at St. Sebastian, the rehab facility.

Apparently, her lack of response to the first letter hadn't stopped Sean from trying to reach her again.

For some crazy reason, Matt felt sorry for the guy. He still remembered the day he'd tried to apologize to Dave, Cindy's ex-husband. Matt hadn't been able to go to the funeral they'd held for both Cindy and Tommy, but he'd called Dave, tried to apologize for...

God, he couldn't even say what he'd actually been sorry for. His competitive spirit? The need to win at all costs?

But Dave had lashed out at him in a fury of grief and pain, leaving Matt to choke on his remorse.

Matt glanced back at the letter and tapped the corner on his open palm.

What had Tori's brother done? Had it been so bad that she couldn't forgive him?

If there was something Matt understood, it was being sorry and not being granted the forgiveness he desperately needed.

The fact that Sean was in rehab told Matt that he was at least trying to make some changes in his life. And that it was likely his drug or alcohol addiction that had been a contributing factor.

With his curiosity mounting, Matt pushed the chair away from the desk and carried the letter out of the office.

"Tori?" he called.

"I'm in the family room."

He took the letter to her, where she was dusting the bookshelf. She watched him enter, then blessed him with a pretty smile. For a moment he thought about backpedaling and not pressing her about the letter. But maybe if he knew what her brother had done he would understand.

So he held up the envelope. "Lester brought the mail. This came for you."

She stiffened, the dust cloth dangling in her hand.

When he gave her the letter, she scanned it briefly, then shoved it into her apron pocket.

"Aren't you going to read it?" he asked.

She studied him for a moment, as though she meant to tell him he was butting into something that didn't concern him. And he would have understood if she'd actually said that. Instead, she said, "Not now. Maybe later."

"Why do I get the feeling that you might never read it?"

She shrugged.

About the time he thought she might not provide him any more answer than that, she placed the dust rag on the shelf, then climbed down from the stool on which she was standing and made her way to the sofa, where she took a seat.

Matt recognized the cue and took a seat beside her, close enough to touch, yet keeping his distance.

"My brother had a drug problem," she said, "but no one told me. I guess they thought it would just magically go away if he left town. So, one day he called and asked if he could move in with me for a while. I figured if he got away from my grandmother, he'd grow up and become more responsible than he'd been in the past. So I said okay."

Matt continued to sit, to listen.

"Not only did I provide him with a place to live," Tori said, "but I also got him a job at the hospital where I worked."

Matt would have done the same thing for either Jared or Greg. "What happened?"

She blew out a sigh. "He got involved in drugs again and stole some pain medication from the hospital. The police were called, and an investigation led to him. They got a warrant and searched my house from top to bottom, finding his stash in his bedroom."

"That must have been tough for you."

"I was devastated and embarrassed. Plus it took a while for me to convince everyone that I didn't have anything to do with the theft."

"Is that why you left the hospital?"

"It was part of the reason." She blew out another sigh, yet kept those other reasons to herself. "I'll probably forgive him someday. But I'm not ready to do that yet. Not until I know that his efforts to clean up and be a responsible citizen are sincere."

"He's in rehab," Matt said.

"I hope that helps, but I know for a fact that he's got a long road ahead of him."

"Would it hurt to answer his letter?" Matt asked.

"Yes," she said. "It hurts whenever I think about the police rummaging through my house, my drawers. And it still tears me up inside when I think about sitting on the sofa of my living room, cuffed like a common criminal because they came to search *my* house because of my brother's drug addiction and theft. Then I was called into work and officially reprimanded for not seeing the signs of his addiction. I nearly lost my job over it all, so I'm not eager to set myself up as one of his enablers again."

Matt could understand that.

But he also knew how it felt to be on the other end, to be the guy wanting to be forgiven.

"My younger brother and sister were spoiled rotten by my grandparents," she added. "They've been allowed to believe that only their wants and desires count. That no one else matters. In the past six months both Sean and Jenna betrayed me one way or another. And I would have never done to them what they did to me."

As the tears welled up in her eyes, Matt reached for her, drawing her close and holding her while she cried.

His heart went out to Tori for what her brother had put her through, but he couldn't help believing that some people ought to get a second chance.

Matt certainly wanted one.

Whether he deserved it or not.

Tori had just finished washing the dishes after the noon meal when Granny and her entourage returned from the city. They entered the house through the back door, loaded down with bags.

Even Connie, who brought up the rear, had her hands full.

"That was fun," Granny said, as she pulled out a kitchen chair and sat down. "Do you want to see all the stuff we bought?"

"Sure." Tori folded the dish towel she'd been using and set it on the counter. Then she watched as the smiling trio spread their purchases across the antique tabletop, displaying school clothes and supplies for Joey, a couple of toys and some pants and tops for Connie.

"Look at my cool backpack." Joey's eyes lit up as he showed her how each zippered pouch worked.

"That's really neat," Tori told him.

Granny furrowed her brow and scanned the doorway that led to the rest of the house. "Where's Matt?"

"He's been working in the office," Tori said.

Granny seemed relieved. "Did you two enjoy having some peace and quiet while we were gone?"

Tori's cheeks warmed, and she hoped she wasn't blushing. "It was all right."

When Joey went to put his things away in the bedroom he'd once shared with Sabrina, Granny excused herself to go to the office and talk to Matt, leaving Tori and Connie alone.

"I really wish Granny hadn't insisted upon buying me those maternity clothes," Connie said.

"From the look on her face, I'm sure she enjoyed being able to do that for you."

"It just seems weird for an employer to be so kind and generous to her employees."

Tori smiled. "Granny isn't like anyone I've ever met."

"I agree. And although I haven't had much experience in the workforce, this job has been a real godsend."

Tori glanced at Connie's tummy, at the pooch that had begun to form. She suspected Connie's options had been somewhat limited with a baby on the way. "When are you due?"

"Around Thanksgiving."

Tori and Connie had been chatting more lately, and it seemed only natural to ask some of the questions she'd had. She was curious about Connie's history and couldn't help envisioning how much fun it would be to have a newborn during the holiday season. "Is your family nearby? With the baby coming, I'm sure that time of the year will be even more special."

Connie placed an elbow on the table and propped up her chin as though trying to decide whether or not she could trust Tori with the details of her past. "They don't know I'm pregnant, and I'm not planning to tell them."

"Ever?" Tori asked, thinking Connie would have to either give up the baby or never see her family again. A child didn't seem like the kind of thing that would be easy to hide indefinitely.

"Well, I'm not going to tell them for a while. The baby wasn't the only reason I left home. My mom…well, let's just say she's ultraconservative and has a high-profile job. Having an unwed, pregnant daughter would be a huge embarrassment for her."

Too bad Tori's brother and sister hadn't given any thought to the embarrassment their choices and behaviors would have on her.

Rather than say anything, Tori studied the attractive, quiet-spoken cook. She'd had her hair cut while in the city. Had she wanted to get rid of the blond highlights that had been growing out?

Or did she just like short hair?

Either way, there had to be a whole lot more to Connie's story than she'd let on, because Tori thought that most pregnant women would want to be close to their mothers and their families at a time like this.

"It's not unusual for a single mom to raise a child on her own these days," Connie said. "And it's really not so frowned upon in our society anymore. But I wasn't supposed to let this happen to me."

"So you're sure your family won't be supportive?" Tori asked.

"No. I'm afraid they would only be disappointed if they knew. So I left them a note about needing to find myself and left town."

It didn't sit right with Tori to think that Connie would have to go through labor and delivery alone.

"How long can you keep the baby a secret from your parents and your immediate family?" Tori asked.

"My family and their disappointment weren't the only reasons I left." Connie combed a hand through the spiky strands of her hair as though she was trying to get used to the shorter length. "I'd rather not go into the rest of it, but let's just say that I learned a very painful lesson about letting my hormones rule my head."

She was talking about the baby's father, Tori realized. "Does he know you're pregnant?"

"No. And I don't intend for him to find out—ever."

Tori didn't know what to say. To her it seemed only fair to tell the man about the baby. But she supposed that was Connie's decision to make.

Still, there was also a practical consideration Connie

should keep in mind. "I guess that means he won't be sending you child support."

"No, the baby and I are on our own." Connie sighed. "But I'm sure everything will turn out okay."

"You don't sound completely convinced."

"I'm sure it will be tough financially." Connie gathered up the bags she'd carried inside. "But the baby's father had a violent streak that I hadn't known about. And I won't live like that. I want to raise my child in a loving, peaceful environment."

Tori could certainly understand that. She'd seen women who'd come into the E.R. battered and bruised by the men who'd sworn to love, honor and cherish them. And she admired Connie for getting out of an abusive relationship before it worsened.

"Have you ever gotten involved with a man before you got a chance to really know him?" Connie asked.

Matt came to mind.

Tori had certainly gotten to know him. And she doubted he had an abusive bone in his body. But she had to admit she'd jumped into a sexual relationship. Especially when she suspected she was feeling more for Matt than he was for her.

A lot more.

"I can certainly see how it could happen," Tori said.

"Hindsight is wonderful, isn't it?" Connie smiled wryly. "If you'll excuse me, I'm going to put these things away, then get started on dinner."

Alone in the kitchen, Tori's thoughts returned to Matt, to all they'd shared last night.

She might have initially made love with him thinking that it was a brief affair, but now she knew differently. She was falling in love with him and wanted their relationship to last.

The problem was, she didn't know how Matt felt about anything long-term. Or about her.

Of course, what did she know about real love anyway? She'd only had one, ill-fated romance in the past.

Matt, by his own admission, was far more experienced than she was. And even if he were open to them having more than an affair, was he the kind of man who could limit himself to one woman? After all, he'd been the kind of man who had dated several women at once.

Sure, he'd been honest with them. But would he revert back to his old ways again once his body had healed?

Was Tori simply part of his healing process?

But what about Cindy? a small voice asked. Matt had made a commitment to her.

Yes, he had. But he'd loved Cindy. And Tori had been a convenient replacement.

She blew out a weary breath. They sure had a lot working against them, not to mention the biggest hurdle of all.

How could Tori compete with the memory of the woman Matt had loved and lost?

Matt was in the office when the call from the title company came in.

Six weeks ago, Granny had sold some property in Las Vegas to Dazzling Desert Ventures, a limited liability corporation owned by some casino bigwigs. From what he understood, the escrow was due to close any day.

The woman introduced herself as Tamara Aguilar and asked to talk to Mrs. Clayton.

"She's not available," Matt said.

"Then is Matthew Clayton there?" the woman asked.

"Speaking." Matt sat back in the desk chair, the springs squeaking.

"Mrs. Clayton gave me permission to discuss this escrow with either you or Jared, so I wanted to let you know that we closed this morning and the funding will take place late this afternoon."

"That's good to hear," Matt said. "Do you have the information needed for an electronic transfer to Mrs. Clayton's bank account?"

"Yes, I do."

Matt thanked her for the call and had no more than hung up when a rap sounded at the door. Before he could invite in whoever had knocked, his mother entered and left the door open.

"Hey," he said, looking up with a grin. "I didn't know you were already home. The title company just called and said the money should be in your account before the end of the day."

"That was quick." Granny took the seat across from him. "I've been talking to Grant Whitaker, my accountant, about the best way to invest that money. I don't suppose you'd mind calling him and letting him give you his thoughts on it."

"Not at all." Matt knew Granny had decided not to reinvest the money in a 1031-exchange by purchasing another piece of property. Instead, she would take the hit and pay the capital gains tax, which would be substantial. But there would still be millions left to invest in other ways.

"I don't know if I told you," Granny said, "but Sabrina won't be coming back to work at the Rocking C. She's going to stay on at Jared's ranch with him."

Matt already knew that after talking to Jared at the party. "I figured you were going to need a new book-keeper. Jared took a hard tumble for Sabrina, and when she was here for your birthday, she seemed just as starry-eyed to me as he was."

Granny winked and pointed her finger at him. "You should be so lucky, Matthew."

He scoffed, yet for some reason he felt a bit hypocriti-cal for his reaction—especially when he'd gotten involved with one of his mother's employees, too.

"Would you mind helping me with the bookkeeping and office work for a while?" Granny asked. "I'd like to have someone I trust. And your math skills have always been good. Besides, you know the ins and outs of ranching."

That was true. And while the offer was both flattering and sound, he struggled with the fact that by accepting the job, he would be accepting his physical limitations and settling. That he'd finally have to come to grips with the fact that he would never ride in another rodeo, never hear the roar of the crowd, never feel the adrenaline rush.

"Sure," he said, trying to muster some enthusiasm in his voice. "I'll help out—at least for the time being."

"I was also thinking," she said, pausing as though wanting to gather her thoughts.

Uh-oh. Granny had a way of orchestrating things to go the way she wanted them to. And while it was known throughout the community that she had a good heart, she also could be cagey when she set her sights on something.

Matt crossed his arms and waited to hear what she had to say.

"Well, Aquila and the foal she's carrying got me thinking. We've always focused on cattle, which is our bread and butter. But I wouldn't mind raising some horses, too. Would you be interested in partnering up with me?"

"You'll be eighty years old next weekend," Matt said. "Why get involved with breeding horses now?"

"Because Everett always wanted to diversify his interests and raise cutting horses. Buying a few good broodmares would be a fitting way to invest some of the money we got from his Las Vegas property investment."

Granny chuckled, then added, "Heck, I might even fancy having a Thoroughbred or two. Can't you just see me hobnobbing with those fancy folks who are involved with horseracing? I sure can."

"Are you kidding?" The word slipped out before Matt could catch them. Was she serious? It wouldn't be the most unpredictable thing she'd ever done.

"It's not a joke. But since you're the one with all the knowledge about horses, I wanted to run the idea past you. I'd also like you to be involved." She slowly got to her feet. "So give it some thought, will you?"

"Sure." As he watched his mother leave the room, he spotted Joey walking down the hall.

The boy paused in midstep, then turned and entered the office. "Hi, Matt. I wish you could have gone with us to Houston. It was really fun."

"I'm glad you had a good time." Matt returned to his work, hoping the kid would think he was too busy to chat.

"Did Sabrina call while we were gone?" Joey asked.

"No, not that I know of."

"Oh." Disappointment seemed to hang on that single utterance.

"What's the matter?" Matt asked, unable to ignore the boy's needs.

"I was hoping that Sabrina would have some good news about my dad."

As much as Matt wanted to cut the conversation short, he couldn't help sympathizing. Joey had lost his mom about six months ago, and his dad was in prison. Matt didn't know many of the details, just that Jared and Sabrina were both convinced of the guy's innocence.

So in spite of his resolve to steer clear of Joey, Matt set aside the invoices he'd been sorting through and gave the boy his attention. "I'm sure she'll call as soon as she knows something definite."

"Yeah. I guess she will." Joey nibbled on his bottom lip, his brow furrowed. "It's just that my dad didn't do anything wrong except try to save a guy's life. And I think he should get a medal or something for that."

"What happened?" Matt asked, wondering what the boy's spin on it was.

"My dad was in his rig when he saw some guys beating up another trucker. So he jumped out to help. And then the men started fighting him. One guy got hurt and died, and my dad got blamed for it."

Matt wasn't sure of all the particulars, but according to what he'd been told, a witness or two who could exonerate Joey's father from any wrongdoing had come forward.

"When my dad gets out, Jared is going to give him a

job on his ranch," the boy added. "So then my dad won't have to drive a truck and be gone all the time."

If there was one thing Matt and his brothers had learned while living with Granny, it was that a guy deserved a second chance.

His thoughts drifted to Tori's brother, a young man who'd definitely made several mistakes. But wasn't the fact that he was in rehab a sign that he wanted to straighten up his life?

What if Matt's uncle had entered rehab? Would Matt's early years have been brighter and more loving?

Kicking an alcohol or drug addiction had to be tough. And Tori's brother was going to need all the help and support he could get.

"Well," Joey said. "I'm going to visit Pumpkin and Fur Ball and the other kittens. See ya later, okay?"

"Yeah. Sure." Matt watched the boy go.

He wondered if he ought to talk to Tori. He didn't want to press her into doing something she wasn't comfortable doing.

But heck. She'd been pretty brutal when it came to pushing him to do the right thing.

In retrospect, he supposed he ought to thank her for that.

And in this case, maybe turnabout was fair play.

Chapter Twelve

That evening, after dinner, Matt grabbed his cane and asked Tori to go outside with him. Apparently, since their nightly strolls had become a habit, no one seemed to give it much mind.

But he'd really begun to look forward to their time together. And he couldn't help wishing they had one more night with the house to themselves.

As they started along the graveled drive, Matt studied the darkened, star-speckled Texas sky, a view in which he'd begun to find comfort. The moon was half its size tonight, only a piece of what it could be.

Just like me, Matt thought, pondering all he'd had to give up over the years.

When he was a kid, he'd lost his biological mother to death and his father to desertion. Then Granny had stepped in, offering him a second chance at love and family.

Maybe that's why he sympathized with Tori's brother, why he thought the guy ought to be given another chance—if he was truly trying to turn his life around.

For some reason, even though Matt didn't know Sean McKenzie from Adam, he felt drawn to the man's cause.

He'd be damned if he knew why it was so important, though.

As Tori walked at Matt's side, he slid a glance her way. Maybe there was more to it than that. Maybe he just needed to know that Tori was the kind of woman who would give a deserving man a second chance.

Since Matt could no longer fall back on his rodeo laurels, he'd have to build another life for himself—a lesser life, one in which his shortcomings would surely come to light.

And if he were involved with a woman…

Again, he stole another peek at Tori.

Hell, he had no idea what was going on between them, but it seemed to be more than just great sex. And if something more serious developed, he needed to know she'd be able to forgive him if he messed up. Because if he couldn't trust her to do that, he wouldn't let things go any further between them. He couldn't.

So in a weird way, Matt had a vested interest in Sean's recovery from addiction.

And that's why he felt compelled to quiz her about her brother, to ask why she wouldn't even read his letters.

It was a touchy subject, though. So he had to think of a way to casually bring it up. While he pondered an opening remark, she beat him to it.

"Tell me about Cindy," she said.

Matt didn't mind talking about his past, but Cindy was the one topic he hadn't wanted to discuss. Yet for some reason—the moon, the summer evening…

Heck, maybe because of the intimacy they'd shared the night before and he hoped they would share again, he decided to answer.

"Cindy was actually the ex-wife of one of the other guys on the circuit."

"Was he a friend?"

"Not exactly. Dave and I were competitors, and while we interacted at various rodeos, we really didn't socialize."

"So how did you meet her?"

"She was visiting a ranch where a buddy of mine had been staying."

She paused before asking, "Were you responsible for their divorce?"

"No. I've got a lot of faults, but dating married women isn't one of them."

Of course, there had been times when Matt had suspected Cindy still felt married to Dave, even after their divorce had been finalized.

"Dave hadn't treated her right," Matt added, more for his own sake than for Tori's. "Cindy hadn't been happy."

"Was Dave abusive?" Tori asked.

"Not physically. But he was gone a lot. And he cheated on her."

Tori seemed to flinch, although he couldn't be sure.

"Some men are weak," Matt said, thinking about the bunkhouse wisdom Clem, the old ranch foreman, had shared with Matt and his brothers.

Listen up, boys. If you marry a woman, then you damn well better honor those vows.

I'd never trust a man who cheated on the person who was supposed to be his life partner and his best friend.

If a man would screw over his wife, what makes you think he'd be any more loyal to you?

"Cindy must have been special," Tori said, drawing Matt from his musing.

"Yes, she was." She'd been quiet, gentle and a good mother. In fact, there'd been something maternal about her that had fed his soul. And he suspected that, deep inside, he knew she'd make a good wife.

"It's funny," he added, "but a lot of people thought we weren't suited. She wasn't like anyone else I'd dated."

"I guess that says a lot," Tori said. "You had plenty of women to compare her to."

She was right about that. Matt had met his share of rodeo groupies—buckle bunnies—who'd wanted to latch on to him because of his fame. Women whose names had blurred with the night like the scenery out the window of a fast-moving train.

Yet for some reason he didn't particularly miss that part of his life. And he'd be damned if he knew why.

Tori continued to walk on his left, the side not depending on the cane. When her arm brushed against his, his hand slipped into hers, and he gave her fingers a gentle squeeze.

It had been an unconscious move, one that felt good and right.

"You must have really loved her," Tori said.

Matt had cared for Cindy. That part was true.

He'd also liked Tommy, a kid who'd thought Matt had hung the moon. Of course, part of that reason was because Matt had filled the daddy-void in his young life.

At least, he had until Dave started coming around and asking for visitation.

To be honest, there was a part of Matt that had actually thrived on winning something one of his competitors had lost.

So, he guessed it was fair to say his and Cindy's relationship had been emotionally complicated.

"A single woman with a child can scare off a lot of men," Tori said.

Matt shrugged. "I guess so."

If truth be told, he'd found the idea of a ready-made family appealing. And although he would have had to work through the shared-parenting thing with Dave, which he had to admit also fed his competitive spirit, he hadn't minded.

So when Cindy had suggested marriage, he'd agreed and they'd become officially engaged. But at times Matt had wondered if wearing his ring had been her way of getting back at Dave, at showing him that he'd lost her to a better man.

But had Matt been the better man?

He'd once thought so.

Now as he looked back upon that last day of Cindy's life, he knew differently.

That fateful Sunday afternoon, her family had shown up at the park for a picnic reunion, which she'd insisted Matt attend with her.

Dave had been an old neighbor of Cindy's and a

friend of her brother's. So when asked to drop by, he had.

But Dave's presence made Matt uneasy and, true to form, Matt had been determined to be one up on the man each chance he got.

Cindy seemed not only uncomfortable with the competition, but annoyed by it. She insisted they leave, and on the ride home, her anger and disappointment permeated the cab of the truck.

As they traveled along the county road near her house, two drag racers came barreling down on them out of nowhere. With only a split second to make a decision, Matt turned the wheel to avoid a head-on collision, opting to run into a ditch. In an attempt to get out of the way, one of the racers turned off, too, and the resulting collision had proved fatal.

Tommy was killed upon impact, and Cindy died while Matt held her hand. She'd asked him to see to it that Tommy was put in his father's care, and he agreed.

He hadn't had the heart to tell her that the boy hadn't made it.

Matt suffered a broken hip and multiple fractures in both legs and ankles. From the beginning, doctors had been unsure as to what extent he would recover, but either way, he would never compete in the rodeo again.

The old Matt would have fought and jumped at the chance for physical therapy and rehab, eager to show them they were all wrong, but the old Matt no longer existed after that horrible day.

While grief and his own guilt had been enough to bog him down, that wasn't even the half of it.

Dave, who was grieving over the loss of his son and ex-wife, stopped by the hospital and lashed out at Matt, blaming him for the accident. "If you hadn't been such a jerk, Cindy wouldn't have insisted on leaving."

The additional guilt was staggering, and Matt had lost—at least, temporarily—the will to push himself, the will to get better.

Why did he have to stir up things with Dave at the picnic? Why hadn't he been more considerate of Cindy?

As Matt's legs began to ache, drawing him from the dark memories, he slid another glance at Tori.

She, too, seemed lost in her thoughts and probably hadn't noticed Matt's lapse into silence.

Tori glanced ahead, noticing that they'd walked farther than usual tonight.

"Are you okay?" she asked. "Do you want to turn around?"

"I'm all right, but I *would* like to head back. I didn't realize we'd walked so far."

Then, obviously his mind had been on something—or rather *someone*—else. And she didn't need a crystal ball to know who that someone was.

He had to have been thinking about Cindy. With a loss that great, that heartbreaking, he'd probably needed some quiet time with her memory.

Still, he continued to hold Tori's hand in a warm and steady grip. Why was that? Had she become a replacement for Cindy?

Of course, she hadn't felt like a replacement last night. In Matt's arms she'd felt like the only woman in the world.

Had she been? Was it possible?

Or had he honed that particular skill after having had his share of lovers?

"You know," he said, "I think your brother and I have something in common."

She tried not to bristle, but she didn't think she'd succeeded. "What makes you think that?"

"I know what it's like to want someone's forgiveness and not receive it."

Was Matt thinking about Cindy again? Did he blame himself for her death?

"Something tells me that Sean may be suffering, too," he said.

"That's the idea. Haven't you ever heard about tough love?"

"Yeah, I've heard about it."

They continued their walk toward the house, the light at the end of the barn illuminating their way.

"Showing Sean tough love might be the right thing to do," Matt said. "But if you've turned your back on him out of anger, it's only going to eat away at you both. And anger can be just as crippling as guilt."

He remained quiet for a while as they walked along the side of the barn.

Tori forced herself to consider Matt's words and try to look at the situation from his point of view. She supposed it was possible that Sean was truly remorseful for what he'd done. After all, he was seeking help for his addiction, since he was still at St. Sebastian's. But it was more complicated than just trying to forgive Sean. She couldn't do that without forgiving her sister. And she just wasn't ready to do that yet.

The intern Tori had been dating—oddly enough, his name didn't come so quickly to mind these days—had represented the future she'd wanted for herself. And so had her job at Lone Star General.

Now, thanks to both of her siblings' selfish acts, along with the public knowledge of them—the whispers and knowing looks—Tori had quit her job and walked away from it all.

Matt gave her hand another light squeeze. "I think we've both had enough serious talk for tonight."

"You're right."

Matt's lips twisted in a little-boy grin, and his mood lifted. "So if you have trouble sleeping in the middle of the night, feel free to sneak into my room. I wouldn't mind having you warm my feet."

"Just your feet?" she asked, trying to play along when she wasn't sure if she actually should.

He slid an arm around her and pulled her close. "Honey, you can warm anything you want."

Matt had lain awake for hours last night, listening for footsteps, for the sound of his doorknob turning. But he'd waited to no avail; Tori hadn't shown up.

Not that she'd promised to, but his invitation and her acceptance had certainly been implied.

Hadn't it?

He supposed there were a hundred reasons she had remained in her room. She could have fallen asleep before the rest of the house had gone to bed.

Or maybe she'd really meant it when she'd said she didn't want a long-term relationship. And she'd suddenly decided that making love two nights in a row was getting in too deep. Or that it might send the wrong message.

Then again, she might have gotten annoyed with him for butting into her business and suggesting that she forgive Sean.

He wished he knew.

But then at breakfast, when she'd asked Matt if he wanted her to drive him to Wexler for his physical therapy appointment this afternoon, he'd figured she couldn't be too angry.

Still, he'd declined her offer.

"I've decided to drive myself this time," he'd said. "But don't worry. I can handle it. Besides, it'll be good for me to venture out on my own."

She'd managed a smile, so he hoped she was okay with him shutting her out, but he had an errand to run today and didn't want her to ride along with him.

So, after grabbing a couple of pieces of toast and a cup of coffee, he'd headed to the office, where he did an Internet search for St. Sebastian's in Houston. Then he studied the Web site, reading up on the rehab center's program, their approach, their success rate.

Yesterday, when contemplating his reasons for being supportive of Sean, he'd neglected to admit one thing that might have been obvious to Jared, who'd had to put up with Matt those first few months after the accident.

While Matt had been recovering at his brother's ranch, he'd hit the booze pretty hard. The only way he'd been able to sleep at night was to drink himself numb. And while his dependence had been circumstantial and he didn't believe he was an alcoholic, he could certainly see how someone who was hurting emotionally could rely upon drugs or alcohol to ease their pain until they were hooked.

So, after finishing all the pending office work, Matt had taken the ranch pickup to Wexler and had another workout with the physical therapist. Then he'd driven to St. Sebastian's in Houston.

It hadn't been as easy to see Tori's brother as he thought it would be, and there'd been a bit of a wait. But eventually, he introduced himself to Sean McKenzie, a young man in his early twenties with short dark hair, green eyes and a ready smile.

Matt mentioned that he was a friend of Tori's, although he hoped that was still true after Tori found out about his visit to meet her brother.

Interestingly, Sean seemed pleased to meet Matt. And he didn't hold back any punches when he talked about the path to his addiction.

"Losing our parents was tough," the younger man said. "And then, six months later, my grandfather was diagnosed with cancer. Tori was in college at the time, and my grandparents didn't want to stress her out, so they kept a lot of that from her. But it got pretty bad. Grampa was really sick with all the chemo they gave him."

"I've heard it can be tough," Matt said.

"You know, it wouldn't have been so bad if there'd been a chance he could have pulled through. But looking back, I think he was trying so hard to live—even if it was a matter of six months or a year—so he could be a dad to us kids. He fought both the disease and the agony of the treatment when most people in his situation would have just accepted that their time had come."

Matt hadn't realized that Tori had dealt with her own share of guilt. She hadn't mentioned anything about the loss of her parents or her grandfather. He was beginning to guess that her way of dealing with grief was to bottle it up inside—just like him.

"I hurt so bad," Sean said, "but I couldn't cry. So no one knew what I was going through. And I couldn't seem to tell anyone that I was dying on the inside. My grandmother tried her best to help, but she was dealing with her own grief. She'd lost both a son and a husband in a very short period of time. So she gave Jenna, my younger sister, and me way more freedom than she should have. I can see that now, even though I couldn't back then."

"When did you start using drugs?" Matt asked.

"At first, I took the leftover pain medication that had been prescribed for my grandfather. But when that was all gone, illegal drugs were easier to get. Because I wasn't using it for recreational purposes, I figured that I would be able to kick the habit when the pain went away."

"But the pain never went away," Matt said. "Did it?"

"No, because I never allowed myself to go through the grieving process."

Sean seemed to be learning a lot about himself, about his addiction. And Matt suspected there was a good chance that his sobriety would last.

"Tori said she got you a job at the hospital where she worked." Matt hated to pry, but he needed to know more about how Sean's decisions and drug use had directly affected Tori.

The younger man nodded. "I swear, Matt. I moved in

with her to try and kick my habit. I figured that if I got out of town and the environment I'd been in, if I met new friends, that it would be easier. And in that sense it was."

"How did you get access to the drugs at the hospital?" Matt asked.

"There was a nurse I'd been dating who had a problem. It's weird how addicts seem to find each other." Sean blew out a sigh. "Anyway, she's the one who had access to the meds, and she got some for me. But I'm afraid I was the one who got caught."

"She didn't?"

"I heard they eventually investigated her, too. But at the time, I thought of her as a friend and didn't want to get her in trouble." Sean raked a hand through his hair. "In retrospect, I should have blown the whistle on her. Her drug problem was risking the lives of the patients she took care of."

"How's the rehab working out for you?" Matt asked.

"Good. *Real* good. In fact, I've decided to go back to school. I want to counsel others when I get out of here. I've really learned a lot."

"Your sister ought to be happy to hear that," Matt said.

"I hope so. I love my sister. She was always good to me. And I'm really sorry about the embarrassment I caused her."

"I'm sure she'll come around," Matt said.

"Me, too. But either way, I'm facing the consequences for the bad choices I made."

The men shook hands, then Matt left the center, climbed into the truck and headed home.

No matter what Tori's decision would be, he was glad

he'd come, glad his decision to support her brother had been validated.

He just hoped that when he told her what he'd done, she'd be okay about his visit to meet Sean and see what he could do to facilitate peace.

Because if she wasn't, if she couldn't see any reason to give her brother a second chance, Matt wasn't sure he could risk laying his heart in her hands.

Tori had gone through the motions today, washing windows and cleaning out closets. She wasn't sure why Matt had wanted to drive to Wexler by himself, and she'd been disappointed when he'd made the announcement.

For a while she wondered if he was angry at her.

She supposed he might have been expecting her to come to his room last night. And she'd actually thought long and hard about slipping into bed with him after the house was quiet.

But while talking to him about Cindy last night and realizing how much he'd loved her, she'd actually been jealous.

Jealous of a woman who'd become an angel in Matt's eyes. How was that for pinning her heart on an impossible dream?

She couldn't help thinking that Matt's misery had been caused more by the death of the woman he loved than the loss of his rodeo career. So she'd decided it was best not to get any more involved with Matt than she had already.

Glancing at her wristwatch, she realized it was nearly five o'clock. Where was Matt? His physical therapy appointment should have been over hours ago.

She strode to the living room, then pulled back the curtain to peer outside.

There was still no sign of him.

Just as she was about to lean away from the window, she spotted the truck coming down the drive.

Relief rushed her chest. Thank God he was safe. In spite of wanting to remain cool and detached, she went to the door and stepped onto the porch.

As he climbed from the pickup, he spotted her watching him and smiled. Her heart clenched as he grimaced in pain, but she knew better than to fuss over him. He'd been clear about that.

And look how independent he'd been today. He hadn't even wanted her to go with him.

Maybe he was pulling away from her, from what they'd shared.

Yet as much as that possibility hurt, she realized it might be for the best.

"Where have you been?" she asked.

"Were you worried?" His face lit up as though her concern mattered, and for a moment she couldn't help believing that there was actually a chance the two of them could become a couple.

"Yes, I was."

He removed the cane that had been lying across the truck seat, then closed the door and made his way to the porch.

"I don't know how you're going to feel about this," he said.

"Feel about what?" she asked, clearly at a loss.

"I drove into Houston and met your brother."

A knot formed in Tori's gut. "You did what?"

"I went to see Sean." He leaned against the porch railing. "He looks good, Tori. And he seems to have his feet on the ground."

Matt might have thought he was being helpful, but an overwhelming sense of betrayal poured over Tori until she found it hard to breathe. Had Sean told Matt about Jenna and James? Did he know that her sister had made a play for Tori's lover?

"You had no right to interfere," she said.

"You're right. But I did it anyway."

Her hands clenched and unclenched, as her anger heated to the boiling point. "I can't believe this. You didn't want me interfering in your life. So how could you do that to me?"

"I only wanted to help. I had a feeling your brother was remorseful, and I believe he's truly sincere. He's been sober for two months, and he's trying to put his life back in order."

But what about Tori's life? How was she supposed to go back to Lone Star General and ask for her job back? And even if she wanted to work at another hospital, she'd still need to provide a reference from her previous employer.

God only knew what had been written in her file.

"Is it that hard for you to forgive someone?" Matt asked, his brow furrowing, his gaze intense.

His question had the effect of a big index finger jabbing her chest. But instead of recoiling, it made her want to stand tall. To fight back.

It wasn't as though she would never forgive her brother. She just needed some space and time to heal, to sort through her options, to replot her future.

"What's the matter?" Matt asked.

"I don't appreciate your going to see my brother. Are

you planning to go back to the hospital and try to get my job back for me, too?"

"Did they fire you?" he asked.

"No. I quit."

"And instead of being the nurse you were meant to be, you prefer to hide out on a ranch instead."

"So what?" she asked, the Irish blood in her starting to rise, her defense on the alert.

He might claim to be trying to help, but she knew what he was really doing. He was chasing her off, just as he'd tried to do with Joey. She'd gotten too close, and he preferred to grieve for Cindy rather than risk loving again.

"You're running away from your troubles," he said, his expression suggesting he'd had a lightbulb moment. "Just like you accused me of doing."

She was running away?

Right this minute she didn't give a rip whether Matt had a point or not. Instead she was trying to regain her footing and decide how to deal with what he had done, what he'd meant to do.

"My career was taken away from me," he said. "But you just threw yours away."

He was encouraging her to get on with her life so she would get out of his.

Well, maybe she'd just make it easy on him.

"I think we need to put some distance between us," she said, trying to garner her pride. Trying to rein in the love she'd felt for him and to protect her heart from breaking any further.

He just stood there, leaning on his cane, and studied

Chapter Thirteen

Matt drove back to the three-bedroom stucco house he owned on the outskirts of Houston. He hadn't been home since before the accident and it showed.

The five-acre property looked deserted and was in need of a good weeding, something he'd have to hire someone to do tomorrow. He'd also have to get the sprinklers going.

It was time, he decided, to face the past, as well as the future.

Walking away from Tori had been one of the hardest things he'd ever had to do. And it had hurt like hell.

After they'd made love, he'd hoped to be able to cut bait before his heart got involved, but apparently it was too late for that. On the way home, as he'd struggled with his emotions, he'd realized that he'd already fallen in love with her.

her as though he had a big decision to make. Finally he slowly nodded. "You might be right."

Then he headed into the house, letting the screen door slam behind him.

Ten minutes later he'd packed an overnight bag, then he limped out the front door and headed toward the pickup.

Tori knew she might be able to stop him.

Instead she let him go.

Some men might not give a rat's hind end about second chances. But they mattered to Matt.

Not that he planned to do anything that needed to be forgiven, of course. But if he did, he didn't want his errors held over his head.

When he was a kid, his uncle used to do that to him. He'd start by bawling out Matt for some childish indiscretion, like spilled milk or whatever. But then he'd start bringing up past grievances, and a beating would follow.

That's why Granny's kindness had been such a soothing balm. And that was why Matt had needed to know that Tori had a forgiving nature before he could consider making any kind of commitment to her.

He chuffed. A commitment. Funny he should ponder one when she hadn't even implied that she wanted one.

As he unlocked the door and let himself into the house, he was met by a wallop of stale, musty air.

The plant Cindy had given him, once green and lush, still sat on the glass-topped table. But now it was withered and dead, a testament to what he'd once had and lost.

"You need a little life and color around here," Cindy had said two days before the accident, when she'd adorned his living room with the potted plant.

She'd been right, Matt thought, as he scooped up the pot, his motion raining dead leaves onto the table.

Then he carried it into the kitchen and tossed the whole kit and caboodle into the trash.

Next he opened the windows and turned on a couple of fans. With that done, he made a quick scan of the house.

On the dining room table, surrounded by a layer of dust, a pile of mail awaited his attention.

Jared must have stopped by while Matt had been in the hospital and collected it from the mailbox that stood in lonely vigil at the road in front of the house. This stuff had probably arrived before his brother had asked to have Matt's mail forwarded to Jared's ranch.

As Matt thumbed through the stack—a lot of it junk that he would toss—he spotted a letter addressed to him.

It was from Andy Thompson, the kid who'd caused the accident.

Not long ago, the teenager had written to tell Matt how sorry he was. But Matt hadn't responded. How could he forgive the kid, when he couldn't even forgive himself?

This letter must have come first, he realized, as he set it aside—unread.

Then his movements froze. He'd been asking Tori to do something he hadn't been able to do.

His sympathies shifted to the sixteen-year-old kid whose stupid decision proved to be a fatal mistake. And he understood Andy's need for absolution.

Heck, Matt would have given anything to hear Dave say, "I know that the accident wasn't your fault." But Dave had lost his only child and his ex-wife, a woman he'd never stopped loving. And, apparently, it helped to have someone to blame when he was hurting, which was a real bitch, as far as Matt was concerned.

And as far as Andy was concerned, too, he supposed. So he tore open the letter and read the kid's words:

Dear Mr. Clayton,
    You have no idea how sorry I am about that

accident and the loss of your loved ones. I am so sorry that I can't eat or sleep.

My parents and the attorney for our insurance company advised me not to contact you, but I just couldn't help it. Will you please forgive me?

Andrew Thompson

Matt blew out a weary sigh. Then he dug through the cupboard in the hutch until he found a notepad and pen.

He might not be able to convince Dave to forgive him for the part he'd played in the tragic accident, but he didn't have to harbor that same, hard-hearted spirit.

As he began his response to Andy, the emotional millstone that had been tied around his neck began to loosen and lift.

His words were short and right to the punch. "Andy, you're forgiven. Enjoy dinner and sleep well tonight. Matthew Clayton."

Then he addressed the envelope, placed a stamp on it and carried it outside, walking along his own driveway tonight, instead of Granny's.

It was a lonely stroll without Tori at his side. But it was a necessary one to make, because as he placed the letter in the mailbox and lifted the red flag, he felt a hell of a lot better than he had in months.

When he returned to the house, he turned on the radio, hoping the noise would lift his mood and help him to shuck the loneliness that had dogged him while he'd been outside.

As a hit by Toby Keith ended and another song began, Matt recognized Greg's voice. His brother sang a ballad about love lost and found, of second chances and new beginnings, and Matt's eyes grew misty. He swiped at them with the back of his hand.

There was one more apology that needed to be made, as well as one more confession.

And it couldn't wait until morning.

When Connie called the household to dinner that night, Tori passed, thanking her but saying she wasn't hungry.

"Where's Matt?" Connie asked.

"I don't know." Tori's words came out soft and slow, a direct contrast to the ones she'd shared with Matt earlier. But with each minute that he'd been gone, her anger had been dissipating.

"Did he ever get back from physical therapy?" Connie asked.

"Yes, but he left again."

"Will he be coming back tonight?"

"I don't think so." Tori's heart clenched at the thought. But she had no one to blame but herself.

A slice of guilt lanced her chest.

She shouldn't have done that. This was Matt's mother's house. If anyone ought to have gone, it should have been Tori.

Besides, she'd begun to see the truth in Matt's words.

She'd let her emotions cripple her, too. She'd been hanging on to her pain, just as Matt had clung to his wheelchair. And she'd refused to do what she could to get better, to heal. She'd been running, too—and not just from her past. In her efforts to escape, she'd nearly thrown away her future—her career as a nurse.

While the others ate dinner, Tori sat in the living room,

an open book in her lap. Yet she wasn't reading. Instead she was listening for the sound of an approaching car in the driveway.

But not just any car, she realized. The pickup Matt had been driving.

Yet the only noise she heard was the tick-tock-tick made by the antique clock on the mantel, reminding her how much time had passed since Matt had left.

If she could wind back the hands, if she could have that moment of confrontation all over again, she wouldn't have been so quick to anger. So quick to defend herself.

Everything Matt had said about her had been right. She'd run away from her problems, and she'd given up the career she loved.

As shuffled footsteps sounded in the doorway, Tori looked up to see Granny enter the room.

"Oh, there you are," the older woman said. "We missed you at dinner."

"I wasn't hungry."

"That's what Connie said."

Tori set the book aside. "Do you have a home phone number for Dr. Graham?"

"I sure do." Granny furrowed her brow. "What's the matter? Are you sick?"

Yes, she was sick at heart. But there wasn't a pill or an injection that could heal that.

"I'd just like to talk to him," Tori said. "That's all."

After Granny gave her the number, Tori placed the call to the country doctor.

"Hello?" the familiar, aged voice said.

"Dr. Graham, this is Tori McKenzie, Granny Clayton's housekeeper."

"Is everything okay at the Rocking C?" he asked.

"Yes, it's fine. But I wanted to talk to you about something. I'm interested in going back to work as a nurse and wondered if you knew of any job openings in or around Brighton Valley. I'd really like to stay in the area."

"As a matter of fact," Doc said, "I've had several conversations with Betsy Bramblett, the latest of which was this afternoon. Dr. Bramblett is a family practitioner in a medical group located in Wexler, and she's interested in buying my practice."

"Are you going to sell it to her?"

"Yes, because I trust that she'll provide the kind of care my patients have come to expect from me."

"Oh," Tori said, her spirits sagging a bit.

"But don't you worry," Doc added, "I just happen to know that Betsy will need a nurse. So I'd be happy to give you my recommendation."

"Thank you, Doc."

"No problem."

When the line disconnected, she felt as though she'd taken a big step in the right direction, yet there was something else that still needed to be done. But that call would need to be made from the privacy of her bedroom.

After closing the door, she dialed information and asked for the number to St. Sebastian's Rehab Center. She was routed to several different people before her brother finally came on the line.

She made an attempt at stilted small talk before getting

to the meat of the matter. "Sean, I'm sorry for not answering your letters. But I want you to know that I support your efforts to get your life back on track."

"Thanks, Tori. I really appreciate that. And I am so sorry for screwing things up for you at Lone Star General."

"I know," she said. "I should have recognized your drug problem sooner. I guess I bailed out on you, Jenna and Gram."

"Hey, I'm learning all about second chances here. And to take one day at a time. So I'm sure things will only get better for our family."

She hoped he was right.

"For what it's worth," he said, "I'm making progress, and I'm assuming responsibility for the mistakes I made."

That was definitely a step in the right direction.

"You know, yesterday in group, one of the guys told the story of a kid who'd played football with him in high school."

Tori wasn't sure where this story was going, but she listened intently.

"The kid's name was Arnie, and each day, after practice, when the guys would go into the locker room and shower, Arnie would just pack up his gear and leave. Whenever anyone asked why he was leaving, Arnie would say, 'I'm going to shower as soon as I get to my house.' But the next day, one sniff told them that he hadn't. One of the guys said that Arnie probably came from a family that didn't make a big deal out of bathing regularly."

"That's probably true," Tori said.

"Yeah, but then my friend in group shared something

pretty profound. Something that really stuck with him and made a point for all of us."

"What's that?"

"Arnie might have grown up in a home where no one encouraged him to bathe. But by the time he was eighteen, he was old enough to know that he stunk. And the only one who could shoulder the blame at that point was Arnie."

"You're right about that," Tori said. "I guess we can only blame others for our shortcomings for so long."

"For what it's worth," Sean said, "Jenna realizes that she stinks, too. And she's making an attempt to take charge of her life. She's been coming to some of the group meetings we have here for the members of our families."

"I'm glad to hear that," Tori said. She supposed she'd have to make a call to Jenna one of these days, too. Not to apologize, but to open the lines of communication between them.

"And that thing with James?" Sean said. "She swears it was only a kiss. And she's not seeing him."

"She needs to realize that women don't do that to each other," Tori said, still angry at the betrayal.

"You're right, sis. But maybe you could cut her a little slack. She lost her mother, remember? And her big sister moved out of the house to go to college. I'm not sure if you knew this or not, but Jenna didn't have many friends. So she's lacking a few social skills."

Sean had a point. Jenna might have been eighteen when Tori had gotten her the job in the hospital cafeteria, but she'd been a baby in so many ways. And while she was wrong for getting involved with James, the intern had been ten years Jenna's senior and had made a commitment to Tori. So, in that sense, he was more to blame than she was.

"Listen," Sean said. "We've got a group session I need to attend, so I have to hang up. But I appreciate your call. And your support."

After promising to visit him soon, Tori disconnected the line and hung up the phone.

But before she could get to her feet and return to the living room, a knock sounded at her bedroom door.

"Who is it?" she asked.

"It's me. Matt."

Tori's heart threatened to burst from her chest. "Come in."

The door creaked open. "I hate to bother you," he said.

"It's no bother." She continued to sit on her bed, her hands resting on the mattress, her feet on the floor, her eyes on the cowboy who'd stolen her heart.

"I came to tell you I'm sorry," he said. "You were right. The decision to forgive your brother is yours to make. I shouldn't have interfered like I did."

"I have an apology to make, too," she said. "For getting angry when you pointed out that I was running from the past. Once I thought about what you'd said, I realized you were right. In fact, I just got off the phone with my brother, and I think I'm going to visit him next weekend. I also called Dr. Graham. He's going to give me a recommendation when I apply for another nursing position."

Matt's grin turned her heart on end. "I'm glad to hear it."

She glanced at the cane he held in his right hand and patted the mattress beside her. "Why don't you sit down?"

"Are you inviting me to share your bed?" he asked, taking a seat.

"Actually, as much as I'd like to make love with you again, I don't think that's in my best interest."

"Why not?" he asked.

She could hold back her feelings, as she'd been prone to do in the past. But she'd begun to realize that no matter how scary or painful they were, she needed to face them head-on. "Because I wasn't being honest with you or with myself when I suggested that we have sex with no strings attached. There's something sacred and safe within those strings. And I'm not going to be comfortable without them."

"Do you want a commitment from me?" he asked, his voice growing somber.

"I realize that Cindy will always have a special place in your heart that no other woman can fill. But I love you, Matt. And if you can't find a little corner of your heart for me, I won't make love with you anymore. I can't set myself up for heartache."

Matt started to chuckle, and she turned to face him, wanting to throttle him. What in the world had he found funny about her heartfelt confession?

When she did, he turned and caught her cheek in the palm of his hand. His thumb skimmed her cheek. "I didn't just come all the way back to the ranch tonight to tell you that I was sorry for butting into your life. I came to tell you that I want you to be a permanent part of mine."

"But—" Tori blinked, trying to make sense of what he was saying.

"There aren't any buts about it, Tori. I love you. And you can have every inch of my heart. It's yours, honey. Now and forever."

Tears welled up in her eyes, and she studied the man

she'd come to love through a watery blur, the man who'd lost the woman he'd loved. "But what about Cindy?"

"I cared about her. A lot." Matt brushed his thumb under her eye, whisking away her tears. "But I don't think it would have lasted."

"The marriage?" she asked.

"No, the engagement. Dave loved Cindy. And the harder he fought to win her back, the harder I fought to keep her. I convinced myself that I loved her, when now I realize what love really is. My feelings for her couldn't hold a candle to what I feel for you."

"Are you sure?" she asked, unable to wrap her heart around his words.

Matt brushed his lips across her mouth, deepening the kiss and showing her just how sure he was.

When they pulled away long enough to catch their breaths, Matt tugged at one of Tori's curls and smiled. "How about coming back to Houston with me?"

"Tonight?"

"My mother might be a romantic at heart, but I'm not sure how she'd feel about us sharing a bed in her house. And since I plan to sleep with you every night for the rest of our lives, I figured we could start now."

"Are you proposing?" she asked.

"I hope you don't expect me to kneel at your feet. But if you'll give me a rain check, I'll ask you properly as soon as my physical therapist gives me an okay."

Tori wrapped her arms around the man she loved. "Then I accept, Matt."

"Excuse me," Granny's voice said from the doorway. "I hope I'm interrupting something."

They both turned to see Granny grinning from ear to ear.

"I might be hearing things, but it sounded as though I walked in on a marriage proposal."

"As a matter of fact," Matt said, "you did. And I hate to be the one to tell you, but you're going to be losing a maid along with that bookkeeper who just gave you his notice."

Granny brightened and clapped her hands together. "I've never been happier to replace a couple of employees in my life. And off the record, that was my plan all along."

"Have you been matchmaking?" Tori asked, stunned.

The older woman's grin stretched across her face, softening her wrinkles. "Now only one of my sons is still unattached, but I hope to get that corrected by Christmas."

And there was just one single, female employee left, Tori realized—unless, of course, Granny had someone else in mind. How many women would set up their sons with a pregnant woman?

Granny leaned against the door. "Have you given that business deal any thought, Matt?"

"Yes, I have." He slipped his arm around Tori's waist. "If you're sure a horse-breeding venture is something you'd really like to get involved with, I'm game. Besides, with my future wife looking for a nursing position in this neck of the woods, it won't do me much good to be based near Houston."

"Good." Granny straightened and took a step backward. "Then I'll leave you two alone so you can plan the details of your wedding."

As his mother slipped out of the room, Matt got to his feet, reached out his hand and pulled Tori to a standing position. "Come on, honey. Why don't you ask Connie to babysit the kittens for us? Then pack an overnight bag, and let's get out of here."

She couldn't think of anything she'd like to do more, but she tossed him a playful smile. "What about those wedding details you told Granny we were going to discuss? She'll probably quiz us on the way out."

"There's not much to talk about." He placed a hand on her jaw, his thumb drawing slow, sensual circles on her cheek, his gaze warming her from the inside out. "You planned one heck of a birthday party that went on without a hitch, so I know our wedding will be the talk of the town. You can call the matrimonial shots. My only suggestion is that we plan to have it in December."

That was six months away, which meant she'd have to get busy and start planning.

"Christmas weddings can be beautiful," she said.

"Ours will be nice whenever we have it, but Greg will be home for the holidays. And I'd like my entire family to meet yours." He brushed a kiss across her brow. "Are you okay with waiting? Otherwise, we can get married right away and plan a reception in December."

"I can wait. I've always dreamed of having a wedding. Nothing big. Just family and friends."

"Good." The love in his eyes filled her heart to the brim. "We can hammer out the other details later. But right now, my mind is in honeymoon mode. And it's a long drive back to Houston. I just hope we make it without having to pull over and find our own little Lover's Lane."

Tori stood and wrapped her arms around the man she would promise to cherish for the rest of her life. "I love you, Matt Clayton."

"I love you, too." Then he placed his lips on hers, claiming her as his own.

Tori wasn't exactly sure what the future would bring, but with Matt at her side, she knew they would weather any storm.

Happily-ever-after didn't start any better than this.

* * * * *

*Don't miss Greg Clayton's story
on sale December 2008.
Available wherever Silhouette books are sold.*

Love Inspired
HISTORICAL

*Powerful, engaging stories of romance, adventure and
faith set in the past—when life was simpler and
faith played a major role in everyday lives.*

See below for a sneak preview of
HIGH COUNTRY BRIDE
by Jillian Hart

*Love Inspired Historical—love and faith
throughout the ages*

Silence remained between them, and she felt the rake of his gaze, taking her in from the top of her wind-blown hair where escaped tendrils snapped in the wind to the toe of her scuffed, patched shoes. She watched him fist up his big, work-roughened hands and expected the worst.

"You never told me, Miz Nelson. Where are you going to go?" His tone was flat, his jaw tensed as if he were still fighting his temper. His blue gaze shot past her to watch the children going about their picking up.

"I don't know." Her throat went dry. Her tongue felt thick as she answered. "When I find employment, I could wire a payment to you. Rent. Y-you aren't think-ing of bringing the sher-riff in?"

"You think I want *payment?*" He boomed like winter thunder. *"You think I want rent money?"*

"Frankly, I don't know what you want."

"I'll tell you what I don't want. I don't want—" His words cannoned in the silence as he paused, and a passing pair of geese overhead honked in flat-noted tones. He grimaced, and it was impossible to know what he would say or do.

She trembled, not from fear of him, she truly didn't believe he would strike her, but from the unknown. Of being forced to take the frightening step off the only safe spot she'd known since she'd lost Pa's house.

When you were homeless, everything seemed so fragile, so easily off balance, for it was a big, unkind world for a woman alone with her children. She had no one to protect her. No one to care. The truth was, she'd never had those things in her husband. How could she expect them from any stranger? Especially this man she hardly knew, who was harsh and cold and hard-hearted.

And, worse, what if he brought in the law?

"You can't keep living out of a wagon," he said, still angry, the cords still straining in his neck. "Animals have enough sense to keep their young cared for and safe."

Yes, it was as she'd thought. He intended to be as cruel about this as he could be. She spun on her heel, pulling up all her defenses, and was determined to let his upcoming hurtful words roll off her like rainwater on an oiled tarp. She grabbed the towel the children had neatly folded and tossed it into the laundry box in the back of the wagon.

"Miz Nelson. I'm talking to you."

"Yes, I know. If you expect me to stand there while you tongue-lash me, you're mistaken. I have packing to get to." Her fingers were clumsy as she hefted the bucket of water she'd brought for washing—she wouldn't need that now—and heaved.

His hand clasped on the handle beside hers, and she

could feel the life and power of him vibrate along the thin metal. "Give it to me."

.Her fingers let go. She felt stunned as he walked away, easily carrying the bucket that had been so heavy to her, and quietly, methodically, put out the small cooking fire. He did not seem as ominous or as intimidating—somehow—as he stood in the shadows, bent to his task, although she couldn't say why that was. Perhaps it was because he wasn't acting the way she was used to men acting. She was quite used to doing all the work.

Jamie scurried over, juggling his wooden horses, to watch. Daisy hung back, eyes wide and still, taking in the mysterious goings-on.

He is different when he's near to them, she realized. He didn't seem harsh, and there was no hint of anger—or, come to think of it, any other emotion—as he shook out the empty bucket, nodded once to the children and then retraced his path to her.

"Let me guess." He dropped the bucket onto the tailgate, and his anger appeared to be back. Cords strained in his neck and jaw as he growled at her. "If you leave here, you don't know where you're going and you have no money to get there with?"

She nodded. "Yes, sir."

"Then get you and your kids into the wagon. I'll hitch up your horses for you." His eyes were cold and yet they were not unfeeling as he fastened his gaze on hers. "I have an empty shanty out back of my house that no one's living in. You can stay there for the night."

"*What?*" She stumbled back, and the solid wood of the tailgate bit into the small of her back. "But—"

"There will be no argument," he bit out, interrupting her. "None at all. I buried a wife and son years ago, what was most precious to me, and to see you and them neglected like this—with no one to care—" His jaw ground again and his eyes were no longer cold.

Joanna didn't think she'd ever seen anything sadder than Aiden McKaslin as the sun went down on him.

* * * * *

Don't miss this deeply moving story,
HIGH COUNTRY BRIDE,
available July 2008
from the new Love Inspired Historical line.

Also look for SEASIDE CINDERELLA
by Anna Schmidt,
where a poor servant girl and a wealthy
merchant prince might somehow
make a life together.

Love Inspired
HISTORICAL

INSPIRATIONAL HISTORICAL ROMANCE

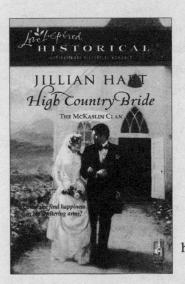

Evicted from her home, Joanna Nelson and her two children seek refuge on the harsh Montana plains—which leads her to rancher Aidan McKaslin's property. When outside forces threaten their blossoming friendship, Aidan decides to take action. Can he convince Joanna to bind herself to him permanently or will it drive her away forever?

Look for

High Country Bride

by
JILLIAN HART

*Available July 2008
wherever you buy books.*

www.SteepleHill.com

Steeple
Hill®

LIH82791

Lawyer Audrey Lincoln has sworn off
love, throwing herself into her work
instead. When she meets a much younger
cop named Ryan Mercedes, all her logic
is tossed out the window, and Ryan is
determined that he will not let the issue
of age come between them. It is not until
a tragic case involving an innocent child
threatens to tear them apart that Ryan
and Audrey must fight for a way to
finally be together....

Look for

TRUSTING RYAN
by Tara Taylor Quinn

Available July
wherever you buy books.

Silhouette®

Romantic
SUSPENSE

**Sparked by Danger,
Fueled by Passion.**

Conard County: The Next Generation

When he learns the truth about his father, military
man Ethan Parish is determined to reunite with his
long-lost family in Wyoming. On his way into town,
he clashes with policewoman Connie Halloran,
whose captivating beauty entices him. When
Connie's daughter is threatened, Ethan must use
his military skills to keep her safe. Together they
race against time to find the little girl and confront
the dangers inherent in family secrets.

Look for

A Soldier's Homecoming

by *New York Times*
bestselling author
Rachel Lee

Available in July wherever you buy books.

REQUEST YOUR FREE BOOKS!

2 FREE NOVELS PLUS 2 FREE GIFTS!

SPECIAL EDITION®

Life, Love and Family!

YES! Please send me 2 FREE Silhouette Speàal Edition® novels and my 2 FREE gifts (gifts are worth about $10). After receiving them, if I don't wish to receive any more books, I can return the shipping statement marked "cancel." If I don't cancel, I will receive 6 brand-new novels every month and be billed just $4.24 per book in the U.S. or $4.99 per book in Canada, plus 25¢ shipping and handling per book and applicable taxes, if any*. That's a savings of at least 15% off the cover price! I understand that accepting the 2 free books and gifts places me under no obligation to buy anything. I can always return a shipment and cancel at any time. Even if I never buy another book from Silhouette, the two free books and gifts are mine to keep forever.

235 SDN EEYU 335 SDN EEY6

Name	(PLEASE PRINT)	
Address		Apt. #
City	State/Prov.	Zip/Postal Code

Signature (if under 18, a parent or guardian must sign)

Mail to the **Silhouette Reader Service:**
IN U.S.A.: P.O. Box 1867, Buffalo, NY 14240-1867
IN CANADA: P.O. Box 609, Fort Erie, Ontario L2A 5X3

Not valid to current subscribers of Silhouette Speàal Edition books.

Want to try two free books from another line?
Call 1-800-873-8635 or visit www.morefreebooks.com.

* Terms and prices subject to change without notice. N.Y. residents add applicable sales tax. Canadian residents will be charged applicable provinàal taxes and GST. This offer is limited to one order per household. All orders subject to approval. Credit or debit balances in a customer's account(s) may be offset by any other outstanding balance owed by or to the customer. Please allow 4 to 6 weeks for delivery. Offer available while quantities last.

Your Privacy: Silhouette is committed to protecting your privacy. Our Privacy Policy is available online at www.eHarlequin.com or upon request from the Reader Service. From time to time we make our lists of customers available to reputable third parties who may have a product or service of interest to you. If you would prefer we not share your name and address, please check here. ☐

SSE08

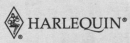

HARLEQUIN®

American ★ Romance®

MADE IN TEXAS

It's the happiest day of Hannah Callahan's life
when she brings her new daughter home to Texas.
And Joe Daugherty would make a perfect father
to complete their unconventional family. But the
world-hopping writer never stays in one place
long enough. Can Joe trust in love enough to
finally get the family he's always wanted?

LOOK FOR

Hannah's Baby

BY

CATHY GILLEN THACKER

*Available July
wherever you buy books.*

LOVE, HOME & HAPPINESS

COMING NEXT MONTH

#1909 IN BED WITH THE BOSS—Christine Rimmer
Back in Business
Little did hotel-chain CFO Tom Holloway realize that his new executive assistant spelled trouble. But even though single mom Shelly Winston was planted by Holloway's worst enemy to take him down, Shelly was no dupe—she had a mind of her own and an eye for her handsome boss.

#1910 DIAMOND IN THE ROUGH—Marie Ferrarella
Kate's Boys
Sportswriter Mike Marlowe wasn't one to pull punches in his newspaper column. So when his barbed commentary about a fallen baseball idol caught the attention of the man's daughter, it meant fireworks. Miranda Shaw would protect her father's name to the end—but would she remember to protect her heart from the cagey scribe?

#1911 HER TEXAS LAWMAN—Stella Bagwell
Men of the West
When someone ran Lucita Sanchez off the highway, it was no accident, but Chief Deputy Ripp McCleod was skeptical of the ranching heiress's story. Soon two things became apparent—someone was indeed stalking Lucita, and Ripp would do anything to protect her as his interest in the case—and the woman—grew very personal....

#1912 THE BACHELOR'S STAND-IN WIFE—Susan Crosby
Wives for Hire
Stalwart bachelor David Falcon needed a woman to administer his household—nothing more. His first mistake—if he wanted to stay single!—was hiring down-on-her-luck Valerie Sinclair. Because in no time flat, David was charmed by this woman and her eight-year-old daughter. Now his bachelorhood teetered on the brink.

#1913 THE COWBOY'S LADY—Nicole Foster
The Brothers of Rancho Pintada
Bull rider Josh Garrett was reckless; shopkeeper Eliana Tamar was responsible. But when fate threw these childhood friends back together, it looked as if Eliana had what it took to tame the wild cowboy...until Josh got a chance of a lifetime to win the title of his dreams. Could Eliana compete with his first love—rodeo—after all?

#1914 THE LAST MAN SHE'D MARRY—Helen R. Myers
After being caught in the crossfire of a troubling case, Texas divorce attorney Alyx Carmel went to regroup at her cousin's house in soothing Sedona, Arizona. Where she ran smack-dab into sexy FBI agent Jonas Hunter, a man she'd reluctantly turned her back on before. But this time, he wasn't taking no for an answer....

SSECNM0608